UNSOILED

THE SMOTHERED ROSE TRILOGY

BOOK TWO

ONE GOOD SONNET PUBLISHING

THE SMOTHERED ROSE TRILOGY: UNSOILED

Cover Illustration and Design by Marrin Sampson,
Interface Graphic Design, Inc.
http://interface-graphic-design.com/

Published by One Good Sonnet Publishing

ISBN: 0993797725
ISBN-13: 978-0993797729

In memory of my mother,
who always saw through
to the beauty within.

ACKNOWLEDGEMENTS

I would like to recognize everyone who has helped me with *Unsoiled*. My heartfelt thanks go out to:

Kitt, whose brilliant eye for story structure and character development will never cease to amaze me.

Marrin Sampson, whose vivid illustrations and cover designs are very much appreciated.

My brother Pete, whose criticisms, though rarely straightforward, were always valid and worth consideration.

My partner-in-crime Jann, whose writing suggestions and assistance with publication and motivation can never be valued highly enough.

And finally, my husband and daughter, who allowed me the precious time I needed to write.

Chapter 1:
Home Is Where . . .

apunzel? You mean lamb's lettuce? Heh. That figures. No wonder sheep are so attracted to you."

Thorny and I were standing in front of the entrance to Silverthorn, the castle which had been our mutual home for what seemed like ages. Though this was the first time I had told him the name my mother had given me, the revelation of my real name wasn't as big of a surprise to him as his was to me. Until the previous night, I had never realized that the wolf named Thorny was actually a magically transformed Prince Thornwald Ashton, heir to the throne of Magnolia.

Everything was further complicated by the fact that

1

I had met him when he was a shepherd first. Now, I had to mentally combine three figures—shepherd, wolf, and prince—into one person, and it was hard. Add to that the fact that he had proposed to me as both shepherd and wolf, and it made for an even more muddled mess.

I felt like I was on the defensive, waiting to deflect yet another proposal from someone I really didn't know that well. I thought Thorny was a great guy, certainly, and we had learned things about each other that perhaps no others knew, but with his real identity having been hidden from me, it limited what I could actually know about him. After all, the questions you would ask a wolf were quite different from those you would ask a fellow human.

Of course, there was also a more logical part of my brain that kept calling me a complete imbecile. As someone who was not of noble blood, I should have leaped at the chance to marry a prince. Love shouldn't have even entered the picture. But ever since my father had gone from wealthy merchant to poor farmer, I could view situations from the perspective of both the poor and the rich. And one thing I knew was I wanted to marry for love.

Oh, I loved Thorny, even if he *had* held me captive, but it was as a dear friend. I wasn't the sort of girl who could fall into romantic love with a beast . . . not to mention the fact that I couldn't help but resent him the whole time I was imprisoned at the castle. Though I might have eventually fallen in love with him when he was a shepherd, I hadn't known him long enough for it to happen. I think all of that was hard for him to understand, and I couldn't blame him. Things were so complicated between us.

"Sheep seemed to like you pretty well when you were a wolf," I pointed out, pushing aside that maelstrom of thoughts to focus on what he had said.

He snorted. "I think they knew that's not what I really was."

I hid a smile. He pretended to despise the woolly creatures, but I thought he secretly liked them. "So you're saying they're smart?"

I could practically hear him squirm. "Nooo," he said uncomfortably. "I'm saying they have animal instincts."

"Do *you* have animal instincts?"

He dipped a hand into the hair behind his ear, looking unsure. "I did, I think. I'm not sure if I do now. I know it was hard holding on to my humanity, even with you there to ground me. Thinking about it all—" He shook his head and huffed. "I'm still pretty irked at my mother for what she did. She should have been more careful when it came to holding onto her own humanity. *Her* physical form was a *choice*. She told me that magic is conditional—you can take on animal properties when transforming or even hurt yourself with your own elemental magic. She should've known better."

"She didn't mean to attack me," I said, and I believed it, though it was still hard to wrap my mind around the fact that the red wolf which had nearly killed Étoile was actually the long-lost Queen Rose. "I don't hold a grudge against her, so you shouldn't, Your Highness." I said this last bit in part to express the truth and in part to serve as a test. The dynamic between us had changed, and I scarcely knew how to

3

act now.

"I have many more reasons than that to hold a grudge against her," he grumbled, but he looked a little less angry. Still, he stared at me for a moment with narrowed eyes and then ducked his head and said, "Don't call me that."

I knew I should have protested—I shouldn't be enjoying camaraderie with a prince—but so much had happened between us that I dropped the formal title without protest. I didn't want him to call me "Miss Beauregard," even if it *was* more proper, and I needed to extend the same courtesy—or lack thereof—to him.

"So your mother can talk to animals?" I ventured.

"Not really. She told me she can mostly just transform into them. And she can see the future." He gritted his teeth at the thought and growled, "Though she doesn't use that second power like she should."

I didn't say anything, not wanting to rile him up further.

We moved toward the fountain that had once held the rose that pulled me into this mess. Though the flower was dead now, I had it in my hair as a reminder of what we had been through. Maybe it was strange, but somehow, it comforted me. And since my father had paid such a dear price for the rose, it didn't feel right to toss it out, even if it wasn't pretty anymore.

"I'm going to miss this place," Thorny said with a sense of wonder, like he couldn't believe what he was saying. "I viewed it as a prison, but now it almost feels like home."

"It's much better than a cave," I said lightly, knowing it could just as easily have been that. If a fairy other than his mother had cursed him, and if he had forcibly ripped me from my home after Nettle had sneered at his appearance, and if the only place he had been able to go was a cave in the woods—

If, if, if . . . I brushed those ifs away. My father once said that ifs were like little bugs that burrowed into your consciousness, but it was only when you focused on them that they were able to eat at you. I thought that was a silly thing to say at the time, but suddenly, I was starting to see the wisdom in it.

"Yeah," Thorny said, sounding distracted. His brow furrowed as he dipped his fingers in the fountain. "Huh?" he muttered, sounding confused. Then he reached in and fished something out.

He held his newfound prize up, water dripping off it to the ground and hitting his boots. It was the magic mirror.

He laughed and shook his head. "I'd forgotten that I threw this in here."

"In a fit of pique?" I guessed, knowing his temper.

"Maybe," he muttered evasively, studying the enchanted object. Then he started shaking it.

"Hey!" I protested as I backed away from the flying water droplets.

He was grinning like an imp. "I thought you liked water."

"Only in large bodies and glasses, thank you."

He laughed for the second time, and I thought about how different it sounded from his laughter as a wolf. It was nice to see him so happy after I had witnessed such moodiness from him. The joy was almost infectious.

"Glad to see *you're* amused, *Thorny*," I said.

"You can have it," he said abruptly, handing the

gilded object to me. "I've had enough of mirrors for a while."

I stared down at it, tracing the intricate patterns on its edges as I thought about the broken mirrors I had seen in Silverthorn. How terrible it must have been for Thorny to be trapped inside the body of a beast. He couldn't read books or even pick up a fork and knife. So many things I took for granted had been denied him.

"Thank you," I whispered.

"Yeah," he said, his hand sneaking into his pocket, likely to touch the letter I had seen him stuff in there. Though he had not told me who wrote it, I suspected it was from his mother. Neither she nor his father had been in evidence in the morning when we woke up. But since Thorny didn't volunteer any information, I didn't ask.

We went to the stables, where we found two horses—Luna and a horse I had seen the day before. When I had arrived at Silverthorn on Luna, I had found the royal huntsman standing outside near three royal mounts—one for him, one for King Oakhill, and one for the body of the king's game. He had tried to keep me from entering the castle, but I had run ahead in a panic and gone to the first place I could think of: my room.

That was where I had found Thorny . . . and where he had almost been killed by his father.

"Looks like the Invis already have our mounts packed for us," Thorny said. He didn't comment on the fact that his father had left a horse behind for him. Maybe that had been in the note.

"The saddlebags look pretty full," I said, eyeing

them.

"My mother says Silverthorn's wealth can't be selfishly taken, only unselfishly given, so I'm giving what I can to your family."

He wasn't looking at me, but I was staring at him. Sometimes, he amazed me. I knew better than anyone how flawed he was—how he could take his selfishness to such extremes as locking a girl up on the grounds of a castle. But even though he, as a revealed prince, must have thought I would soon be betrothed to him, somehow he still remembered the poverty of my family.

"Thank you," I whispered for the second time.

But he ignored my expression of gratitude and said: "Now, we need to get Soleil and Étoile, and then we can go."

I felt my eyes widen in surprise. "But you hate sheep." Allegedly, anyway, though I wasn't about to add that.

"I figure you can lead Soleil on a rope while you ride," he said, yet again neglecting to respond to what I had said, "and I can carry Étoile."

"Are you sure?"

"If the lamb squirms too much, I can stuff her in a sack."

"You are *not* carrying her around in a sack."

He grinned at me.

After fetching the sheep, we left Silverthorn on horseback, with Thorny directing a few mumbled curses at the squirming lamb in his arms. After we had journeyed for a few minutes, the prince commented, "One thing you can't fault my father for is his taste in horseflesh. Even the horse meant to cart my carcass home is a fine specimen."

"Well, I try not to fault my own father for much," I said carefully, uncomfortable talking negatively about the king to his son. "I'm glad to be going home to him."

"Yeah," Thorny said, but he didn't sound especially happy. I got the impression that if he were on the ground, he would be looking down and kicking at leaves like a kid who had been told he didn't get to go to the fair.

Memories of his proposals suddenly filled my head, and I prayed he wouldn't see our brief ride together as a chance to make yet another one. I wasn't ready for that yet. Right now, all I wanted was to enjoy the thought of seeing my father again. I didn't want to be whisked away to another castle by Thorny so soon.

It wasn't the most noteworthy of journeys. We spent much of the time talking, although that was often punctuated by Thorny's struggles with the energetic lamb in his hands. The invisible servants had packed plenty of food, so we took some breaks to eat and let the sheep be together while the horses were given some relief from their heavy loads.

On our last break, I gazed fondly at Luna. I thought she was happy to be out and about. She even seemed to take having Soleil on the ground near her in stride (not that I would have expected anything else from her). Thorny's horse, however, was harder for me to read. All I knew was that he was packed with muscles, presumably for carrying the dead body of a large wolf. The fact that the king didn't succeed in his hunt was nothing short of a miracle.

Of course, though I knew how to saddle and groom and otherwise care for a horse, I didn't know much about judging whether one was valuable or not. When I was wealthy, I had simply chosen a horse I thought was graceful. I was fortunate that she had turned out to be dependable as well, just as I was fortunate that such a great bond had formed between us. Even if that bond, like the rose, was part of the reason I had been held hostage at Silverthorn.

I smiled and gave Luna's nose one final stroke before mounting her for the last leg of our journey.

"You look happy," Thorny observed, gazing up at me from the ground.

My brow crinkled slightly as I noted his guarded expression. "I'm going home to my father. I have my freedom again."

His lips tightened, and he looked almost like he was in pain. But then he masked the expression with a grin, and he climbed up his horse and told me, "Yes, and I'm sure your father will be thrilled to see you, though he might want to take a gun to me. I seem to have that effect on fathers somehow."

I shook my head, not knowing what to say. Times had been pretty tough on us both.

That final leg of the journey was especially quiet for some reason. Even Thorny's curses were muted. But then a familiar house was in sight, and the awkward atmosphere didn't seem to matter anymore.

"We're home, Luna," I whispered into my horse's ear. All the stresses and worries I had been facing melted away. Thorny wasn't my captor, but a friend; Silverthorn wasn't my prison, but a place I would look back on fondly.

"Do you want to go on alone?" Thorny asked. He looked uncomfortable and sad, and I had an inexplicable urge to hug him.

"No, come with me," I said, wondering if he had any other poignant expressions I had missed simply because I wasn't well versed in wolf body language. "I'd like you to meet my father again, now that you're not as frightening."

"You mean ugly," he said flatly.

"No, that's not what I meant, Thorny." I hesitated, not certain whether to elaborate, but then I decided to seize the opportunity to do so. "You know, I saw you outside one night, looking at the moon. The faint light shone down on your dark fur and made it gleam. Somehow, you seemed so forlorn. And rather than seeing you as a vicious beast, in that moment, I began to see you as a beautiful tragic figure. And then I started thinking about how beauty really is in the eye of the beholder."

He laughed, but it was one of those dry, disbelieving laughs. "I never saw myself as beautiful."

"There is beauty in all of us," I told him gently, "but it's the inner beauty that matters, not the outer. I'm sorry it took me so long to see yours."

"Yeah, well, I'm not exactly the prettiest man on the inside, so I'm not surprised." He was trying to jest, but the way he was avoiding my eyes and picking at his clothes made the humor fall flat.

Since the subject made him uncomfortable, I was willing to continue with the humor route. "A man?" I scoffed. "You're only a boy. You couldn't even become king yet if your father abdicated the throne."

"That 'must be twenty-one years old to rule Magnolia' rule is ridiculous. I'm a man in every sense of the word except that one."

I grinned at him. "Whatever. Now, stop delaying. I want to see my father."

After we set the horses up with a ground-tie, I decided to restrain the sheep. While I did consider letting Étoile bound around, knowing she needed to release some energy, I didn't want her curiosity to get her into trouble, so I took the safer route.

Once the animals were secure, Thorny and I walked up to the door of the small house. I reached out and started to turn the knob, but my hand refused to make a twisting motion. It was my home—I didn't *need* to knock—but for some reason I pulled my hand away from the knob and did so. I felt like an outsider trying to be let in. I wasn't sure if Silverthorn had changed me or if the passing of time was causing my imprint to fade from the place, but something made it hard to return, though it was what I had wanted above all.

There was a brief delay, and then my stepmother opened the door, and the smile I had mustered died on my lips. Iris—who always wore bright, eye-catching colors—was clothed completely in black.

"Where's my father?" I said, my mouth dry as a desert. The world wasn't spinning, yet I knew everything was about to careen out of control.

Chapter 2:
Death's Touch

f we had been a normal family, Iris would have hugged me and said, "I'm sorry, baby," before crying out the story in my arms. I would have hugged her back and sobbed on her shoulder. And somehow, we would have found a small amount of comfort in our shared grief.

We weren't a normal family. All she did was pinch her lips together and say: "Oh, it's you. I thought *you* of all people would never have the courage to return here after what you've done."

"Thorny, go," I whispered, my eyes stinging.

But the prince's hackles were up due to Iris's insult, and he took a step toward her and growled: "What's going on?"

"Thorny, go!" I cried out, using more force than I had ever mustered before in my life. It was suddenly imperative that he leave.

I could tell by the way he looked from my stepmother to me that I had hurt him, but he didn't argue. He just gently placed a hand on the small of my back for the briefest of moments, and then he turned and walked away after muttering, "I'll return."

I was finding it hard to breathe. I asked Iris again: "Where's my father?"

"Who was that?" Iris asked, watching Thorny mount his horse. She had a calculating look on her face.

"Prince Thornwald Ashton, heir to the throne of Magnolia and *former wolf holding me hostage*. WHERE IS MY FATHER?"

Even though I was shouting, my stepmother didn't want to take her eyes off Thorny. But finally, she looked at me again, and the expression of interest Thorny had brought to her face changed to one of disgust. "What happened is you killed your father. Now, get out of that ridiculous dress and put on some proper mourning clothes." She waved a hand in the air. "Poppy should help you find something. But I must say that I'm surprised you should condescend to join once more with your impoverished relatives."

She was right that our family was poor. All we should have been able to manage was a black ribbon or two—but there Iris was, wearing a black bombazine silk dress and jet jewelry, looking the perfect picture of a grieving widow. And I would be expected to follow her example, though not so stylishly.

I moved into the house, too dazed to even know

how upset I was. I gazed around hopefully, as if I might find my father hiding in a corner somewhere.

It was a tiny house compared to our old manor, yet it was still bigger than we should have been able to afford. To the right, there was a dining room (my stepmother had insisted on having a place to entertain despite our poverty) and the master bedroom. A bedroom, a closet, and a room with a small tub and chamber pot were situated to the right. Straight ahead was the sitting area, and then further back, against the wall, there was a small kitchen area with a fireplace. Many commoners weren't even fortunate enough to have so many walls.

But I didn't care about all that. I was only trying to concentrate on details to prevent myself from collapsing into a puddle of tears in the middle of the room.

Walking unsteadily, I went through the open door belonging to the small bedroom on the left. The black-clothed Poppy was sitting on the large bed she and I had shared with Nettle. She was mending a dress (*More black,* I thought numbly), and I watched as her hands moved up and down.

When she finally noticed me, the slight frown of concentration turned into a smile.

"Oh, Labelle!" she exclaimed, looking genuinely happy to see me. But then she remembered the circumstances surrounding the meeting, and her brow furrowed once more. She stood up awkwardly, clutching the dress. "Nettle has gone to the market to buy us some food. We—we might not have enough for you. We didn't know that you would be back."

I shut the door behind me with a trembling hand,

not caring a whit about food. Poppy moved forward and embraced me.

"I'm so sorry, Labelle," she whispered.

My chest felt tight, and I wanted to scream. But I had to ask: "What happened to my father, Poppy?" I could still hear his pleas for me to stay ringing through my head. Why hadn't I listened to him?

"Are you sure you want to know?" Poppy asked. She wasn't so bad when her mother and Nettle weren't around. In fact, if it weren't for them, we might have been friends.

But while I appreciated her concern, I needed to know what had happened to my father. I needed to know how he had d . . . I couldn't even think the word.

"Yes," I said.

"I heard them talking to Mother," Poppy said after a short pause. She bunched up the dress in her hands, trying to avoid my gaze but constantly raising her eyes to look at me, as if to make sure I were still there. "When you left again to see that dreadful wolf, your father went to the pub. He started drinking and drinking—and because he knew the pub-keeper would stop him from drinking too much, he started to have other people get him drinks. So nobody knew how much he'd had."

"What next?" I whispered.

"They thought he had fallen asleep, you know? But it was more than that. He—he fell unconscious, I guess, and eventually, they realized that he'd—" She cut off, as if deciding to revise what she was going to say. Finally, she said, "He fell asleep and didn't wake up."

It was like a guillotine had fallen in my brain, severing my connection with reality. My body went limp, and I was on the floor sobbing as Poppy kept saying that nickname that my father had given me. *Labelle. Labelle. Labelle. Labelle.*

It made me think of funeral bells and black clothes and cold dirt. Somehow, I had wrenched the dress away from Poppy, and I was yelling into it. "No! No! Why? Why?"

This was my fault. I had saved Thorny by killing my father.

I could picture my father in that pub, bleary-eyed and guilt-ridden, blaming himself for sending me off to live with a beast. I had tried to tell him that Thorny wasn't the monster he had thought, but to no avail. Maybe if I had taken my father to Silverthorn with me—if I had encouraged Thorny to talk to him. Maybe, maybe, maybe. It was all for nothing.

It wasn't fair! If he could have waited one more day for me to come home!

I suddenly realized I had dug my nails into my palms so hard that they were bleeding. I wiped my eyes and nose on one of my embroidered Silverthorn dress sleeves and thought, *I must not look like a beauty right now.*

I laughed at that, and Poppy, who had been watching me with pity in her eyes, jumped in surprise and gave me a wary look.

"Mourning clothes," I somehow managed, though it was hard to breathe, much less speak. I knew my stepmother wouldn't let me mourn at my leisure. I would have to do the rest of my weeping at night when she was in bed.

Poppy helped me into a black crepe dress that was

a little too short, and then I stumbled out of the room, only to be verbally attacked by my stepmother.

"It certainly took you long enough to put that dress on," Iris snapped. "What a lousy daughter you are, wanting to stay in your pretty expensive clothes instead of showing the proper respect to your father. Always holding your vanity above all, of course. You should be ashamed of yourself."

I stared at her blankly. Nothing she said could make me feel any worse.

"There's a part of me that doesn't want to let you attend his funeral. After all, good daughters don't run off to play with animals instead of helping support their struggling families."

I lifted my head at this. Keep me from the funeral? That thought penetrated the fog that was shrouding my brain.

Iris continued: "Of course, it wouldn't be seemly for his own flesh and blood to be missing at the funeral when she has recently returned from a 'stay with her great-aunt,' so I will let you come, though you certainly don't deserve to be given the opportunity."

I think she was waiting for me to say something— to thank her, most likely—but I just nodded. I felt as if there were a storm tossing everything around me up into the air, and all I could do was watch helplessly as my knees grew weaker and weaker.

Iris's lips pressed together a little more tightly. "I've been thinking about what to do with you now that you're back. You need to take over all the cooking, of course, and we'll expect our meals to be punctual, flavorful, and frugal.

"That won't take much of your time, of course,"

she continued. "Most of your day will be spent in the field. And after working outside, you are to clean the house. You can start by regularly cleaning the fireplace. I can't stand a filthy fireplace." Her mouth was a thin line now.

I thought numbly of how I always associated her with pursed lips and the phrase "of course." *Of course your father's gone,* I thought to myself pathetically.

And then she was saying that phrase again: "Of course, you should have saved us all a lot of trouble and gotten yourself eaten by that prince when he was a wolf. But I suppose royal tastes are better than that." Maybe she was joking, and maybe she wasn't, but there was no trace of humor in her voice.

I did think, however, after looking closer, that her eyes seemed red, like she had been crying a lot recently. And then I felt another pang of sorrow in my heart. I knew she had married my father for his money, but she had grown to love him in her own way. She had simply always hated me because my father had loved me more and valued my beauty above hers. Her displeasure when I left Silverthorn to visit my father for a week had been quite obvious . . . as had her pleasure at parting ways once more.

She had every right to hate me now. I was the reason my father was dead. I deserved any punishment she threw my way. I would do what she wanted me to, even if it *was* something ridiculous like working in mourning clothes.

When it was finally time for me to go to bed, I was dirty and exhausted and almost didn't make it to the cot set up in the corner for me. I wasn't allowed to sleep with Nettle and Poppy in their bedroom anymore; instead, I was placed near the privy, where the stench of the chamber pot gave me a potent reminder that I had forgotten to dump it. But having grown unaccustomed to such labor meant I was too tired to work any longer. So I simply cried a little into my grimy hands until I fell asleep.

And then I started to dream. I dreamed I was shut in my Silverthorn tower, crying into a pillow. The door opened, and I looked up to see Thorny. He was by my side in an instant, embracing me. "What happened, Elle?" he asked me, with such tender sympathy in his voice that I couldn't help but hug him back.

I was suddenly very glad that he, at least, didn't call me by the nickname my father had given me. In fact, "Elle" was closer to my real name than "Labelle" was.

"I killed my father, Thorny," I told him. It was easy to talk and cry at the same time in a dream. "He drank himself to death because I left him."

Thorny withdrew from my arms and looked at me with a sober face. "He should never have died. I should've been the one to die."

"No, Thorny." I shook my head adamantly. "Neither of you should've died."

He looked away from me. "If my mother had told me your father was going to die, I would've warned you that you needed to stay with him. She should have told me."

"The fault belongs to me alone," I insisted, standing up from the bed and pacing the length of the room, which seemed to be growing longer and longer the way rooms sometimes do in dreams. "He's dead because of *me*!" I shouted.

And then my vanity mirror broke, and I ran to the

pieces and wondered if I could die in real life after being cut by shards of mirror in a dream. I heard Thorny shouting behind me, but I pushed him to the edge of my dream-self's consciousness and lifted a large piece of the broken mirror. There was blood on my hands almost instantly, and when I looked in the fragment I held, I saw my father's face, and I knew somehow that it was his blood.

"I'm sorry," I whispered, but his lifeless eyes just kept staring at me. And then there was a red stream flying out of the mirror and all over my clothes and my face and my hair, and I stood there, unflinching, waiting for more to come.

Thorny intruded on my consciousness again with a shout: "Elle!"

And I yelled back: "Go away, Thorny!"

The mirror fragments exploded, and I woke up.

I was still on my cot, but my face was buried in my hands, which were wet with tears. I grabbed my thin blanket and lowered myself off the cot to the cold floor. Then I stuck my head beneath my cot and cried into my blanket until I was asleep again. But at least that time I didn't recall any dreams except for the vague memory of an image of my father's face in a broken mirror growing larger and larger.

CHAPTER 3:
CINDERBELLA

My stepmother let me go to the funeral.

A few generations ago, women weren't even allowed to attend funerals. It was supposed to be too much for their delicate sensibilities or something like that. But now they were expected to be there. It was deemed necessary for closure.

But standing outside in the grass, staring down at the long and plain wooden box holding the body of the man who used to be my father, I didn't feel anything like closure. All I felt was the constant pain that had become my invisible companion. It was beyond tears. It was an aching emptiness. Maybe the ache would someday subside, but the emptiness could never be filled. I knew that, and no funeral could shut off my awareness of that part of me.

Thorny was at the service, too. I saw him from a distance. But when our eyes met, I tore mine away, and he didn't approach me. I was thankful for that.

He did come to the house later that day, though. I was working in the kitchen when there was a knock at the door, and my stepmother answered it. I don't know what I would have done if she had asked me to do it. Broken down in an ocean of tears probably. I'd had to force myself to cry at the funeral—it was expected—but my emotions seemed to come in waves of extreme numbness and extreme sorrow. Right now, it was the latter.

"Umm, hello, Mrs. Beauregard. Can I speak to Elle—umm, Labelle?" Thorny asked.

"I am so sorry I cannot grant you that request, Your Highness, but she is indisposed at the moment," said Iris without missing a beat. "Would you like to see my daughter Nettle instead? I can assure you that she is excellent company."

"No, uh," he said, sounding flustered, "that's all right. I'll come back another time."

"Well, I am so sorry to hear you can't stay," my stepmother said.

Thorny mumbled something before presumably walking away.

I heard Iris shut the door and come up behind me. While I could have honestly claimed I hadn't turned to watch their exchange, it was best for me to pretend that I hadn't heard what they said either. So I acted like I didn't know she was there.

"Thankfully, I answered the door instead of you," Iris said abruptly, and I pretended to be surprised as I turned to look at her. "Of course, it goes without saying that I don't ever want you answering the door again. You are much too filthy to present yourself to visitors."

"All right," I said. It wasn't as if visitors were knocking down our door anyway. The only person in our family that had been any good at making friends was my father, and he was gone. I felt my eyes fill with tears.

Oblivious to my sorrow, my stepmother suddenly began to laugh.

Her laughter filled the room, a titter that ascended into a cackle and then fell to a mere chuckle. The effect was somewhat manic, and it was enough to jolt me briefly out of my misery.

I looked at her as I wiped my eyes, wondering if it was my sorrow she found amusing. But though I felt that she wasn't laughing at me, I couldn't figure out what it was she found so funny.

Moments later, her eyes seemed to clear, as if she were coming back to herself. "Oh, by the way," she said suddenly, as if nothing out of the ordinary had happened, "there's one more thing. I've got a letter for you from your father. Let me fetch it."

I stood there waiting as she went to her room to get the letter. My concerns over her random laughter fled, to be replaced with something not unlike hope. My father had left words behind *specifically for me*? My heart pounded in my chest with anticipation.

When Iris finally returned with the piece of correspondence, she thrust it at me. "Read that," she ordered. "Then return to work." With a haughty sniff, she walked away, leaving me standing there with letter in hand. I thought I might have heard her laugh again, but I quickly turned my attention to the letter she had given me.

The words on the ratty piece of paper were disappointingly brief and not filled with the sentiments I had hoped would be present. The letter said simply:

Labelle,
If you ever return, you must help your stepmother. She needs you. This is all I ask of you, daughter.
Your Father, etc.

I stared at it for several minutes, willing other sentences to appear. I wanted to ask my stepmother for more information—when had my father written the letter? Was this his dying wish?

I took in a broken breath. Did it matter? He was gone now, and if he had wanted this from me, how could I deny it to him? Clutching the paper to my chest, I resolved to do as he had asked. It was the least I could do after having driven him to his death.

The next few weeks were a blur of work. Nearly every day, my schedule was the same. I would make breakfast and a sack lunch for everyone, and then I would collect eggs and go milk our cow before turning to the hard work of farming. When darkness approached, I left the field to make dinner. I served my family in the dining room, ate a quick meal by myself, and then cleaned the house until I couldn't hold my eyes open anymore. Despite my stepmother's obsession with cleanliness, rarely was there an opportunity for me to even wash my own face with a rag.

One night, I was cleaning dishes when Nettle came over to criticize me. She and Poppy never did any work after the final meal of the day, and they often left the house entirely for a few hours after dinner to do who knew what. This night, however, both of my stepsisters had stayed home.

"The fireplace is dirty again," Nettle said. She had picked up on her mother's preference for a spotless fireplace in spite of the fact that we rarely had any visitors. "You need to scrub it till it shines." Never mind that such stones never would actually shine, no matter how hard I scrubbed them.

"Yes, Nettle," I said. I didn't meet her eyes. She would just think I was challenging her.

After finishing with the dishes, I went to the fireplace as she wanted, trying to clean every nook and cranny since I knew it would be inspected afterward. All the while, Nettle's eyes were boring into my back.

Then, so suddenly and loudly that I jumped, Nettle said: "Look, Poppy! It's Bella of the Cinders. She certainly doesn't look like 'The Beauty' now, does she? Not with that rat's nest of hair or those filthy chicken arms. Maybe we should start calling her 'Cinderbella.'" Nettle started laughing as if she had said the cleverest thing in the world, and I heard Poppy weakly join in.

I didn't look at them; I just continued cleaning the ashes and soot, aware that it was on my face and hands and clothes, aware that the picture I made was a far cry from the beauty my father had always praised. Why should I have cared whether or not my hands were soiled with soot? What need did I have for beauty anymore?

But as I scrubbed, my hands raw and quite possibly bleeding from overwork, I couldn't stop my eyes from burning with tears. I felt like a plant that had been uprooted and tossed to the ground and trampled on. Or maybe more than that—a plant that had been wrenched from the soil and flung into a roaring fireplace, with nothing to anchor it to the world or even provide protection from the blistering heat and nasty ashes.

I knew it was partially by choice. How could I forget that Thorny was continuing his attempts to see me? Iris and my stepsisters always turned him away, saying I was busy or gone, and while that was often true, still he kept coming. Of course, my stepsisters, never as busy as I was, got enjoyment out of his visits even if I didn't, for they always found some excuse to go outside for a few minutes to watch him walk away as they giggled over his tight breeches or his expensive coat.

But regardless of how many girls were eyeing him, I knew he, prince though he was, would sweep me away from this place and help remove the filth from my hands if I only gave him the word. But I didn't want him to do that.

The letter I had received bound me to this place. I had to respect my father's wishes. A part of me feared I even deserved to be punished for his death. There must have been something I could have done that would have led to both him and Thorny surviving the night. But I hadn't done it. And that was something I had to live with.

In spite of these feelings, I did allow myself one pleasure. I had hidden the mirror that Thorny gave me, and every night before I went to sleep, I looked in it and asked to see Thorny.

He was always asleep before I was, and that was fine with me. It was comforting to me to see his peaceful face and know that he, at least, was still alive. It was like the flicker of a candle in a dark room—not enough to warm you, but enough to keep you going.

To say I was miserable would be to call a cloud "cotton"—you would be sort of close to the big picture, but there would be something you weren't quite grasping . . . something you *couldn't* grasp. Not unless you knew what it was like to be unable to clean up the grime that coated you from head to foot—and what it was like for your limbs to always be aching from exertion. Or even the way it felt to keep thinking about how the place where you lived could never be a home without your father's presence to brighten it.

I had these thoughts in my mind especially strongly whenever I milked my family's cow, Ciel, as it was work that didn't require mental effort on my part, and my mind always wandered. But one morning, when I was hunched down, doing that very task, a shadow fell on me, briefly clearing my brain of all its troubles.

I looked up and nearly fell off my stool in surprise when I saw who it was.

"What are you doing here, Thorny?" I whispered, glancing around, certain that Nettle or Iris would be popping out of the ground somewhere to scold me.

"I've been trying to see you," he said, sounding annoyed, "but your stepmother keeps trying to convince me you've fallen off the face of the map."

"You need to go," I said, resisting the urge to push him away . . . and the urge to embrace him and never let go. "If my family sees the two of us talking, they'll kill me."

"You'd think you would be happy to see me," he said, crossing his arms and showing no indication that he was about to leave.

"I have a lot of work to do, and my stepmother doesn't allot time for chatting." That sounded nastier than I had meant it to, but I was tired and more than a little panicked.

While Thorny narrowed his eyes, he was obviously trying to remain unfazed, as he continued calmly: "I thought I'd let you know I'm staying at an inn here in New Fountain—and I have been since the day we arrived. But more importantly, I wanted to make sure you're still alive before I return to your house tonight."

I frowned and looked at him in suspicion. "What do you mean?"

He gave me a grin that lit up his face and made me realize just why Nettle and Poppy liked to gush over how handsome he was. "Oh, I'm coming to dinner," he said, and then he swaggered off.

I stared after him, slack-jawed and feeling as if the wind had been knocked out of me. My stepmother had actually given him permission to eat with us? Or was he planning to just show up? Even with all the presents from Silverthorn that he had sent, it was hard enough for us to feed ourselves, much less another person, as my stepmother hated to sell even a single pretty item—not to mention the fact that everyone in the village knew we were still nose-deep in debt.

Yet though I felt like protesting, my mind was drawn even more to the mystery of what had brought this on. There was no way Thorny was oblivious enough—or stupid enough—to show up unannounced and expect to be fed. He must have talked to my stepmother when I wasn't around. After all, what better prize for Nettle could there be than a prince looking to wed someone? Yes, that certainly made sense. I could already visualize my stepmother's face as she worked out all the details of that union and what it would mean.

But I didn't know why he actually expected to see me at the dinner. I usually took my meals quickly after everyone else had eaten; Iris and Nettle never wanted me, filthy as I was, to sit at the table *with* them. I sincerely doubted Iris would suddenly lift her ban of me from the dinner table to allow me to interfere with her plans for Nettle. Thorny was going to be disappointed if he expected a pleasant evening where we were able to talk and catch up on everything we had been doing since we parted ways.

I tore my thoughts away from the prince with some difficulty—he really had looked roguishly handsome with that grin on his face—and hurried to finish the milking. I needed to get back to the field. Luna and I had a lot of work to do still, and my stepmother wasn't one to tolerate excuses. There was no sense in thinking about the prince's soft brown hair and intense green eyes and strong hands . . . or even the way the corners of his mouth crooked upward when he smiled. No, I needed to focus on my work. Iris would be appalled if she knew I had taken even the briefest break from my duties.

For some reason, however, I was having a difficult time concentrating, and it showed in my terrible job milking. But Ciel, sweet as she was, simply looked at me and mooed.

"Sorry, girl," I muttered. Why had Thorny felt it necessary to show up anyway? And why couldn't I keep him out of my mind?

CHAPTER 4:
OF SWORDS AND SALADS

efore the dinner with Thorny, Poppy and Nettle flitted here and there amid giddy giggles and hushed whispers and swishing skirts. Iris let them put on some of their finest gowns (Poppy had to wear black, but Nettle was allowed to push the boundaries of proper mourning "just this once"), and though the dresses may not have fit them perfectly, still my stepsisters would have made a great showing at any social event.

Nettle had black hair and fair skin like her mother, and both always caught appreciative eyes. For this dinner, her hair was swept upward and sprinkled with pearls that Iris had somehow held on to despite the debts hovering over our heads. There was a matching necklace, and add to that a magnificent lavender gown, and Nettle looked radiant.

Poppy's light brown hair was intricately arranged into a careful sea of curls. Her dress was not as fine as her sister's, but she also looked stunning.

I wasn't even given a chance to clean myself, much less change. Iris had evidently weighed the pros and cons of my being presentable against my looking like a servant girl and decided in favor of the latter. She herself, of course, was immaculate.

When Thorny arrived, I was told to open the door (as was befitting of a servant girl). He had a single red rose in hand, and when he saw me, he faltered. I felt like crying suddenly, but I kept my face blank with great effort. He looked so handsome in his dark blue coat, tan breeches, and perfectly tied white cravat, and I suddenly understood better how he had felt as a wolf. The transformation from this picture of male beauty to that of a beast must have been quite a shock indeed.

He started to say something, but Nettle swept forward, saying, "Don't keep our dinner guest waiting, Cinderbella, dear." Then she laughed and took the rose from Thorny, whose barely restrained anger called back to my mind the wolf he once was. "Thank you so much, Your Highness. Please, enter our humble abode. Labelle will take your hat."

They moved to the dining room as I took care of Thorny's "traveling" items. It seemed absurd to keep up even a pretense of such high-class civility when coming to eat dinner at this particular household, but Thorny had probably been missing the trappings of his station while he was a wolf since all he could wear was a silly black cape.

Once I entered the dining room, Iris gave me a sharp cue, and I served everyone their first course before she gestured for me to sit down myself. The rose, I noticed, was in a vase at the center of the table. While my appetite had all but fled, I forced myself to take a bite before looking at Thorny, whom Iris had placed as far from me as possible.

His face was growing stormy, and his fingers were digging into the table almost like claws, but I gave him a quick shake of my head and hoped he understood my message. If he yelled at my stepfamily, it would make things worse. *He* wouldn't have to deal with the aftermath of his actions, but *I* would.

"You have such big strong arms, Your Highness," gushed Nettle, eyeing them. "Is that from practicing swordplay?"

"No, it's from hauling sheep around," Thorny said curtly. I knew that wasn't true—it was more likely that his present musculature was somehow developed during the time he had spent as a wolf *chasing down* animals, not picking them up—but I didn't say anything.

Poppy was more subtle in her flirting. "But you must polish your big sword a lot."

For some reason, Thorny started choking on his drink. After he finished sputtering, he said, "Swords like the one I, erm, brought don't often get . . . used, so you don't, ah, have to polish them very much." He paused and said lamely, "My sword is very shiny." He squeezed his eyes shut, obviously uncomfortable.

"Can I see your sword?" Nettle asked. She gave him a sultry look and purred, "I'd really like to touch it."

Thorny's eyes shot open, and he turned bright red. "No, ah, swords are too d-dangerous for girls like you. My, this is fine cutlery, Mrs. Beauregard," he said, turning to my stepmother.

She gave him a knowing smile. "You would certainly know, Your Highness. You did, after all, send it home with Rapunzel." She didn't pause or even blink an eye, but I knew that since my father was no longer here, she had realized it was acceptable to downgrade me from "Labelle" to "Rapunzel." Strangely, I didn't mind.

"Uh, yeah," Thorny said, examining his fork. "It does have that Silverthorn look."

"Of course, Nettle can show you the other fine things we have done with your generous gifts. I know you'll find in her bedroom—"

"No!" said Thorny sharply. "I'll, uh, be fine without a tour of the house, thank you."

I couldn't shake the feeling there was something going on that I didn't understand, but I was not about to ask about it, so I simply tried to enjoy the luxury of eating a meal at a slow pace.

After a moment's pause, Thorny began, "So, Elle, have—"

"Oh, Rapunzel isn't much for dinner conversation, Your Highness," interrupted Iris. "Poor simple dear. But Nettle has a very skilled tongue."

"Yes, I am quick to give a good tongue-lashing to any who deserve it," said Nettle with a secretive smile.

Still red-faced, Thorny attempted to address me again. "Elle—"

"Doesn't Nettle look beautiful tonight?" asked my

stepmother. "And Poppy, too, of course. But I always thought Nettle looked especially spectacular in pearls. Of course, she would look magnificent in anything. She seems to belong in a castle, does she not? Wouldn't she make the perfect image of a queen, Your Highness? They would be dying to stamp her face on coins."

Thorny looked over at me, obviously frustrated by my stepmother's interference with his efforts to speak to me. But I wasn't surprised. She had always resented how my father paid so much more attention to my beauty than her own. Of course, her resentment was more than justified, as both she and her daughters were stunningly beautiful. But it was hard to remember that sometimes when she was yelling at me over how I cooked a carrot or cleaned a tile.

"When I'm king," said Thorny, making me think again of how surreal it was that we were having a prince to dinner, "I'm going to do away with that stupid practice of stamping the current ruler's face on coins. I think maybe a magnolia tree on one side and a phoenix on the other should be good enough."

Iris and my stepsisters gasped.

"That's blasphem—" began my stepmother, only to realize who she was talking to and modify what she said to, "Your Highness, umm, are you quite certain?" The first name of the man who had founded Magnolia's rival kingdom was "Phoenix." Though Magnolia was not currently at war with Airland, cavalierly discussing Airland at the dinner table was frowned upon.

Thorny crossed his arms. "Without Phoenix, Hawthorn would never have founded Magnolia.

There's nothing wrong with honoring our forefathers."

"I don't know that I would call the dead Landdish King our forefather, Your Highness," Iris said stiffly.

Nettle took a bite of food while giving Thorny a wary sideways look. Meanwhile, the prince smirked at me. I could practically see his thoughts: *See? I shut them up.*

But then, after a few moments of no sound but that of silverware clinking against dinnerware, Poppy asked innocently, "Are you *sure* you don't want to show off your sword?"

"I'm sure," growled Thorny.

"You have impeccable style, Your Highness," Nettle said, placing her hand over his arm. Though he snatched his arm away, she acted as though she hadn't noticed. "But I think you would look good in anything. Don't you agree, Poppy?"

"Oh, yes, definitely," Poppy said.

His face cloudy, Thorny lifted up a fork and turned it over in his hands. "Oh, that's not true. I look pretty beastly in sheepskin."

Nettle tittered as though he was making a joke, but I saw Poppy glance at me. She looked slightly troubled.

Apparently, Iris also picked up on the fact that they were now treading dangerous waters, as she said, "Of course, I am certain an understanding and generous prince such as yourself would not try to blame my daughters for anything they might have said while you were a wolf. Such enchantments are hard to penetrate, Your Highness—as I'm sure you know, you were just as likely to be a transformed goblin as a prince."

Thorny's mouth was a thin line. "Elle and her father never treated me badly." That was a downright lie—I *had* treated him badly at first. My only saving grace was that I had never tried to be malicious, as I was mostly afraid of what might happen to me. But I knew that in my fear I had said some unkind things. My father was the only one who had treated wolf-Thorny with any form of civility. I felt my eyes start to burn in shame.

"Oh, you know the sensibilities of ladies, Your Highness," Iris said, trying to play it off. "Even the smallest mouse will send us scurrying from a room."

"My mother had three pet mice," Thorny countered. "Their names were Pumpkin, Coach, and Horse. She let them eat from her palms."

Iris waved her hand in the air with an indulgent smile. "Of course, royalty are allowed their quirks, Your Highness. A queen or king without any quirks would make for a dull kingdom indeed."

Thorny snorted and took a bite of food.

The rest of dinner passed in a similar fashion, with Nettle flirting, Poppy occasionally chiming in, my stepmother trying to promote a union between her eldest and the prince, our guest of honor getting grumpier and grumpier, and me eating quietly. I knew Iris would block any attempt I made at conversation, so I didn't even try. There was no sense in upsetting Thorny even further.

When at last everyone was done eating and we couldn't linger any longer at the table, we moved out of the dining room, and Iris said in a haughty tone: "Your Highness, you and Rapunzel may spend thirty minutes in front of her ashy throne before she has to return to clean up dinner. I am sorry, but we cannot spare her for any longer than that."

I looked at Thorny in surprise, and he stepped toward my stepmother, fire in his eyes. Iris actually took a step backward, intimidated for a brief instant, but she quickly regained her composure. "Actually, Your Highness, now that I consider the matter further, I suppose you might find the crisp night air to be more to your liking. I must admit, however, that I do wonder why a sophisticated man such as you would want to talk to such a filthy girl at all."

"Elle is more beautiful to me as she is now than the three of you combined," growled Thorny. "And I'll thank you to stop insulting her in my presence, *Mrs. Beauregard*. I can always have some of my father's men come collect some of the debts you still owe. I've heard about them in town. People here would take little provocation to jump on you. Especially if they knew about the pearls and nice cutlery you've hidden away."

Iris paled and bobbed a curtsy. "I apologize, Your Highness. Of course, I never intended to offend you. As a sign of my generosity, this once you may take forty-five minutes of Rapunzel's time, though it will be hard for us to lose that much of her work, struggling as we are to make ends meet."

Thorny's face was stone, like this was no more than he expected, and as he gave a curt nod, it struck me that there was something *regal* about it. I suddenly realized that there were many sides to Thorny . . . and that maybe this side truly *was* somewhat appropriate for a future king. After all, part of a ruler's duty was to survive the machinations of the court without making it obvious that manipulation was happening. He had managed to get a sincere apology out of Iris, which was a feat in itself.

Meanwhile, Poppy was offering Thorny his hat, which he placed on his head, and his cane, which he took in his left hand. He put his right arm out, and I, not knowing what else to do, took it in mine and let him lead me outside. There was a strange warmth to his arm that somehow seemed to spread to my cheeks.

"You might not want to show yourself favoring me so obviously," I murmured as the door shut behind us.

"I don't care," he declared, waving his cane in the air. "I want the whole world to know how I feel about you."

"It's just a boyish crush," I said dismissively, removing my hand from the crook of his arm. I took a few steps forward, intending to go to the barn.

But he caught my elbow and turned me toward him. "No," he said, his green-eyed stare so intense that I felt something twist in my stomach, "it's not." His fingers kept their grip for a second more before he released me and started walking again.

It took me a moment to take hold of myself and follow him. I couldn't help but touch the place where his fingers had been, as if I could still feel their heat.

After I followed him inside the barn, we both stopped, and I tilted my head and lifted my shoulders with a sigh. "What are you doing here, Thorny?"

He set his cane down and reached out to pat the unfamiliar horse I assumed was his before moving to stroke Luna's nose. Casually, he took his hat off and set it over one of her ears, but she promptly shook her head, and the hat fell to the ground. Thorny looked down at it for a few seconds, obviously gathering his thoughts, before he finally spoke.

"The only way they'll let me talk to you is if I eat a meal with them," he said, "so we struck a bargain that every night after I do that, I can speak with you in private for thirty minutes. I . . . I have to see you, Elle."

He turned to look at me, and I saw the desperation of a man in love there, and my earlier dismissal of what he felt as being a boyish crush suddenly felt cruel. "I know you can't afford to feed me," he said, "so I'll give you coins every night from a bag my father left for me. I'd give you a lot at once, but I know your stepmother would probably find them somehow—I have the feeling she has a nose that can sniff out anything of value—and I don't want her using them to buy more jewels—"

"Did you mean what you said earlier?" I interrupted.

He frowned at me, trying to figure out what I was referring to. "Oh, you mean about the debts and stuff? I wouldn't ever try to crush your family like that, even if your stepmother is a wi—erm, well, not so nice of a person. And the townsfolk feel sorry for your family. And a little awed, too, on account of how pretty you all are."

I rubbed my chin and looked away. It was a stupid question, but I felt like I needed to know the answer. "No, I meant what you said about me, looking like this." I was covered in dirt and likely smelled of sweat and animals. I bore no resemblance to the girl my father had nicknamed "Labelle." How could he see anything beautiful in me?

"I meant it," he said fiercely, grabbing my left hand with both of his. "I've been shallow most of my life, and that's how my interest in you began, but it's grown into something deeper. Now, seeing you as you are, I love you more, and my heart . . . it goes out to you so much it hurts." He sighed. "I'm not great at this mushy stuff, but I want you to know—no amount of grime can soil my image of you."

It was one of those moments where you expected someone nearby to say, "Aww." And I did feel touched by what he said, so I put my free hand on top of his in response and squeezed. But the gesture made me wince, and Thorny saw it.

He turned my hands palms upward and lifted them for examination. They were red and blistered from constant work, and when Thorny noticed that, his face twisted in anger. "Why are they treating you like this?"

I pulled away from him and turned to look out the open barn door. I could see the red streaks of sunset coloring the sky.

I stared at the colors for a few moments—at the blend of red and orange—and at last, I whispered, "I'm the reason my father's dead." My chest felt tight, and I wanted the ground to open up and consume me.

I felt the prince's hand grip my shoulder. It was not gentle with love, but rough with anger. "It's not your fault, Elle," he said in a low voice. His rage made him sound guttural. "You don't deserve this. I talked to people in town, and what happened to your father, he did to himself."

"He was upset because I left him!" I shouted, shoving Thorny's hand away and twisting to glare at him. "It wouldn't have happened if I hadn't left!"

"And then I would be dead." His anger was gone now, replaced with something like sorrow. "Maybe that would've been for the best."

I reached out to touch his shoulder. "Thorny, that's not what I meant."

He shrugged my hand off. "Look, I get it. You loved your father, and you don't love me."

"I loved my father as family, Thorny—but I love you as a friend. There must have been some way for me to save you both."

"Sometimes, you can't save everyone. But you can save yourself, Elle. Come marry me—maybe you can grow to love me the way I want you to. My mother's disappeared again, and my father doesn't want me to marry you, but we can elope. It—"

"Your father doesn't want you to marry me?" I interrupted. I wondered if that had been mentioned in the letter he had been given at Silverthorn.

"Oh, you know," he said, avoiding the question, "I'm supposed to spend time from age eighteen to twenty-one on princely learning. Etiquette, history, dueling, archery, learning how to rule—all that stuff. If it weren't for my mother, he probably would've dragged me back to his castle and locked me up in a tower until I promised to obey his orders."

I looked down at my grimy black dress. "Your father is right."

"W-what?" Thorny sputtered. "Elle—"

"We *shouldn't* marry. At least living here, even if I'm worked hard and miserable, I know I'm accomplishing something—whether it's gathering eggs or picking tomatoes, I can see the fruits of my labors. And you are the *prince of Magnolia.* You should be off learning more about what's in store for you, and you should do it for the sake of your kingdom. If you were to marry me, people would only see your wife as a pretty face. Thorny, I don't want to be viewed as an ornament for your arm."

"You wouldn't be viewed as an ornament for my arm," he protested. "And if you become queen, you could help your subjects and really accomplish something."

"No, Thorny," I said softly. I felt sorry for him—he was holding on to a dream that couldn't be. I was finally beginning to leave my dreams behind me. They were childish things, after all. I only wished my separation from them didn't hurt so much. "The people would think you were like your father—just marrying a commoner for her looks. They wouldn't respect either of us."

"That's not—"

"It *is* true, Thorny," I cut in. "You don't know how the people talked, because you're not one of them. But *I* am. Maybe I wasn't that old when your mother disappeared, but I had ears, and I remember the things people said. They sneered at both your parents—and they still talked badly of your father even when your mother left him. If she had revealed she was a fairy, maybe people could have respected her. But she didn't, so they viewed her as an uneducated beauty, a commoner with nothing to give and everything to gain by marriage."

"I didn't realize that's how it was," Thorny said softly. He sounded like someone who had just heard news of a small-scale tragedy. And perhaps, to him, it was.

I hated to tell him all this—I was talking about his *parents* after all—but he needed to hear it. And he deserved an explanation for why I couldn't marry him. "As if it wasn't bad enough that your father married a commoner, he had to choose a hunting dog as his Animal Crest. Maybe most people aren't well-versed in the complexities of Animal Crest symbolism, but they all know a king's pet isn't the proper choice for something meant to symbolize his reign. It told them that he wanted to keep to his personal pleasures above all."

Thorny frowned. "I didn't realize people put much stock in that. I thought it was just another stupid tradition."

"Thorny, when you become king, everything you do will be scrutinized. And I don't want to be the reason your people hate you. You should marry a duchess or something. The people need to have faith in their ruler again."

"Elle, I think they would like you—"

"No, Thorny. You just keep seeing what you want to see. You've read too many books and entertained too many fantasies. You have to grow up." I bit my lip and turned away from him. "You shouldn't come here anymore."

I felt him come up behind me and put his arms around me, and something inside me tightened and ached as he murmured into my ear, "I will find a way for us to be together, Elle, and I will still come to see you." He placed a kiss on my shoulder, and then his warmth was gone, and I shivered.

It would be better for everyone if I never saw him again. I knew that. But thinking about it made me so sad that I wanted to hug my arms against myself and sink down to the barn floor. Instead, I watched as he got his cane and hat and then rode his horse off into the night. I should have been upset that he meant to ignore my advice and return. But I wasn't.

CHAPTER 5:

THE ARM OF AVALON

rue to his word, Thorny returned every night. Though dinner was like a circus with a prince as the dancing bear, I began to look forward to those brief periods of conversation with Thorny after the evening meal. That was the one time when my eyes didn't threaten to sting as much as my hands. It was my pleasure with my punishment.

I should have told him more forcefully never to return, and I probably could have convinced him if I really tried. But I liked seeing him, even if only briefly, so I didn't. Still, it made me feel guilty as he continued his attempts to persuade me to elope. Nonetheless, I stood my ground. I knew that option would only end in disaster.

Every day, however, it became harder to get Thorny out of my head. He was becoming ingrained in my life in a way that he never could have done as a wolf. And those thirty minutes a night that I spent alone with him were never completely enough for me, so I kept glancing in the enchanted looking-glass at him every night just to see his sleeping face. But then one day, I suddenly wanted to know what kept him busy during the daylight hours.

When I thought the house was empty, I snuck inside and pulled out the enchanted mirror from under my cot. Gazing into it as I kneeled, I said, "Mirror, mirror, in my hand, show me just where Thorny stands." I didn't need to rhyme like that, but I always felt so strange talking to a mirror that I had begun to add some formality to it.

Thorny's image swirled into view, and I watched as he lifted something. I realized he was helping someone put a wheel on a wagon, and I smiled. It was such an unprincely thing to do, but knowing who he was made it seem that much more powerful an act. Maybe he hadn't learned much about commoners from fifteen to eighteen due to his time spent as a wolf, but he seemed to be learning something now.

"So," a voice said behind me, making me jump, "you've been hiding a magic mirror."

In my panic, I scrambled to hide the object, but my stepmother yanked me up by the back of my dress and twisted me around to face her.

"Good. Of course, that means you should be able to return to the faelanx and get more riches for us. I imagine the place feels an affinity toward you."

"No," I said adamantly, wondering how she could

know so much about Silverthorn. "That wealth isn't ours. Besides, Thor—the prince said its wealth can't be selfishly taken, only unselfishly given."

"The prince," repeated Iris with a curled lip. "Don't think I haven't seen how you look at him. You might as well not even glance his way. I have designs for him and my Nettle, and I won't let some twit of a girl have him, no matter what it takes."

I clenched my teeth together. She was less than sane if she could think that Thorny would ever consider marrying *Nettle*! And as for me, while I had no intention of marrying Thorny, she had made me furious, and I said in what was almost a shout: "He's a free man! He can marry whoever he wants!"

That was the wrong thing to say. My stepmother's beautiful face turned to ice, like a stone-cold statue crafted by a tormented artisan. Then she slapped me.

I brought my hand up to my cheek, still feeling the stinging imprint of her hand. As if anticipating what was to happen next, the fingers of my other hand tightened around the mirror handle.

"Rapunzel," she said, "if there is one thing you need to learn today, it is that either I get what I want, or I make sure no one else does." She gave me a sweet smile that turned my stomach. "And of course, what I want right now is your *mirror*!" This last was punctuated by a jerk of the looking-glass out of my grip, causing me to cry out at the sudden jolt of my arm and the scraping of the mirror's gilded handle on my tortured palms.

I watched as Iris took the enchanted object to her bedroom, a place that was as off-limits to me as a castle with a crocodile-infested moat. This time was different from all the other instances where I had been insulted and abused. This time, she had taken away one of the few items that meant something to me.

Sitting on my cot, I put my face in my hands, my eyes filling with angry tears. Would my father truly have wanted this for me? Had he really believed I was meant to stay here and help such a selfish woman?

Soon, I was crying in earnest, my body shaking with each sob. I didn't even hear the front door open when Poppy came in the house, but I did hear her say my name.

I looked up, trying to dash the tears from my eyes and gain control of my breathing, but it was pointless. Even a child could have seen I was distraught.

"Are you all right?" she asked in concern.

"No," I whispered, burying my face in my hands once more. "I'm m-miserable here."

"Then why do you stay?" Poppy asked softly.

I looked up at her, my whole soul in agony. "Because my f-father . . . w-wanted me t-to. He . . . he l-left me a letter."

She was quiet for a few seconds, a frown on her face, and then she said, "Labelle, that letter my mother gave you was . . . well, it was a fake."

"W-what?" I gasped.

Poppy looked abashed. "I heard Mother tell Nettle she wrote it to ensure you'd stay here. She said it was the least you could do for our family. She didn't want you to leave. I think she just . . . I think she just wants to take all her anger out on you for how things have turned out."

My thoughts were like a charging bull trying to come to a sudden halt. I had been staying here because

49

I thought my father had wanted it . . . but he hadn't?

"You're sure?" I asked. My voice was calm, utterly devoid of the pain that had filled it moments before.

"Y-yes. I'm . . . I'm sorry I didn't tell you before. But . . . but I didn't really want you to leave either." Her face was pink, and she truly seemed regretful.

I didn't care. Perhaps I should have been angry, but I wasn't. I was relieved. The great weight that had been pressing down on me had been lifted.

I didn't have to stay here and take Iris's abuse any longer. I could leave, be free—I could be my own person. My accomplishments no longer had to be measured by what I did to help my stepmother. Instead, if I wanted, I could give myself a fresh start. I could collect eggs from my *own* chickens.

Maybe Iris had taken my mirror, but so what? It didn't matter anymore. A smile spread across my face, and I thought with crude glee, *She can stick it where the sun doesn't shine!*

I could be my own person! The thought was freeing.

Meanwhile, Poppy was staring at me as if I were about to start dancing on tabletops. I simply grinned at her and said, "Thank you so much, Poppy."

After Poppy and I parted, I went back outside the house with a cheery attitude, whistling under my breath as I worked. I was going to create a new life for myself. It was a wonderful feeling.

My mood was broken only slightly when I came across Iris a little while later. She was alone in the house, standing in the doorway to her room.

I paused, hearing her voice, but I soon realized she wasn't talking to me. I frowned, as she was using a fond tone not normally taken on with her daughters, and I took a few steps forward to listen.

"You really can't understand what I'm talking about," she said. "I know, Gaheris, I know."

I started. She was talking to my *father?* Unable to help myself, I moved quietly to a different position in the house so I could see into my stepmother's room. A part of me dared hope . . . but there was no one in there.

"You should have seen what Fennel Maplewood's wife was wearing at the funeral of that poor farmer. It was a ghastly black thing. Even your daughter made a better showing there than she did."

I bit my lip, feeling a brief surge of pity. The only funeral I had been to since I returned home was the funeral of my father. My stepmother seemed confused. I supposed we all had our different ways of grieving. It wasn't so uncommon to speak to a dead loved one.

But though the incident made me feel more kindly toward my stepmother, I was still determined to leave. If I stayed, it would simply make us both unhappy.

When I went out to the barn that night after Thorny performed his usual trained wolf act, my joyful feelings continued. Though spending time with my stepfamily had been wearing on him lately, he also seemed unusually happy. I didn't want to ruin his mood by telling him that Iris had taken the mirror from me.

"I have an idea," Thorny proclaimed as we walked into the barn after dinner. Like he usually did, he tossed his cane and hat aside.

I lifted an eyebrow. "Oh, yeah?" I meant to humor him. That was typically the easiest route.

"We're going to make you the next Queen of Airland."

I stared at him like he had sprouted fur, and I waited for the punchline, only to realize he was serious. "This isn't a storybook, Thorny."

"I'm not a five-year-old, you know," he said, but though he sounded annoyed, he didn't look it. "This is real. Tell me, have you heard of the Arm of Avalon?"

"No, but I have the feeling I'm about to," I muttered.

Ignoring me, Thorny began: "Queen Avalon, the first Fairy Queen and the wife of King Phoenix, had no children or designated heirs. The people loved her, and she always said that they were her children."

"Is there a point to this?" I murmured, not because I was actually bored, but because I wanted to see Thorny's cheek twitch.

"So when her husband died," he said loudly, failing to hide both his annoyance and the twitch in his cheek, "she came up with an alternative to simply choosing an heir from her court. She had a well-known sword that she was so skilled at wielding that it was like an extension of herself, and they called it the Arm of Avalon. In fact, it was while she was training with her blade on the ship-ride to Airland and Magnolia that Phoenix and Hawthorn fell in love with her.

"But it wasn't an ordinary sword; it was a magical one. And she took it to a lake with witnesses from her court and said, 'Whosoever wishes to be the next Queen of Airland must ask the Lady of the Lake for this sword.'

"And then, using the last of her magical strength to imbue the sword with more power, she threw it into the lake, and she collapsed on the ground, dead."

That caused me to raise an eyebrow, but I let him continue.

"They named the lake after Queen Avalon, and they continue the tradition of choosing rulers this way. Some claim the Lady of the Lake is Avalon herself, while others believe it was a different fairy, the one who gave Avalon the sword many years before." Thorny shrugged. "My father says that it's a barbaric tradition and the throne should always go to a monarch's heirs. Often, it does; the former queen's children *do* usually attempt to get the sword. I've asked around some—my dad didn't like talking about Airland much when I was little—and people say the last queen's child died not too long after birth. The Patient Steward is taking care of the throne now—"

"The Patient Steward?"

He shrugged. "That's what they call their regent. Anyway, he's been taking care of the kingdom for well over a decade. Apparently, no one's been able to successfully retrieve the sword from Lake Avalon."

I didn't even try to hide my skepticism. "And you think this is something I can do?"

"Look, it's been years since the last queen's death," he said. "You probably won't even have any competition. Why not take on a quest?"

In spite of his exuberance, I felt one of his primary motives was to get me away from my stepfamily. Even if this sword and lake existed, it was unlikely that I would actually be the one to successfully find both.

But I was ready to stop moping around. In spite of whatever Iris thought, my father would never have wanted me to be Cinderbella. Starting anew in Airland could be just what I needed. I was eighteen, and surely I could find a job as someone's maid or cook. Once we actually reached Airland, I would tell Thorny of my plans and convince him to return home to his father to learn his princely duties. This quest of his was bound to be boring—surely, it wouldn't take too long to persuade him to go. And if words didn't work, I could simply disappear. Prince or no prince, Thorny's authority wouldn't extend to Airland.

"I'll go," I said, watching as a big grin spread across his face. I felt a pang of guilt for deceiving him like this, but I wasn't certain I could make it to Airland alone—not considering all the news of bandit raids on the rise.

"Great!" Thorny exclaimed. "I've got a questing manual that's perfect for the occasion. I've been dying to put what it says to good use. I'm going to go pick up all the supplies for our journey. I'll need about a week to gather stuff—we can't have inferior supplies, after all. We'll need food, of course, and . . ."

I let him ramble on while I thought about what I should do after I reached Airland. The work might be just as intense as that required by Iris, but that would be fine. I would be crafting a new identity as Rapunzel. With a few well-placed smudges and a little careful arranging of my hair, maybe I could ensure that I wouldn't be seen as the Beauty. Everything that had always set me apart from others need not be true in Airland. Maybe I would make some friends. And perhaps someday I would marry a real shepherd who would never have reason to resent me because of our unequal stations. And we would laugh about how I almost married a prince who became a shepherd who became a wolf—and about how ridiculous all that was.

But as I looked at Thorny and listened briefly to him expound on the benefits of a good pair of shoes for questing, I felt a strange pang of something not unlike regret. In spite of his shortcomings, Thorny was a good guy, and he would take the reins of kinghood with a steady hand once he matured a little. I only hoped he would be able to find a good woman to guide him.

As I nodded and uh-huh'ed over his descriptions of our supply list, I failed to realize that this was one of those cases where he *really* needed a more practical hand to stay him.

CHAPTER 6:
WHAT'S LEFT BEHIND

he period during which Thorny was gone on his supply hunt was a trying time for me. A week and a half without the prince was enough to really wear on Iris's nerves, as she had no idea what he was doing and only knew that he was gone. I suspected she feared that he might never return . . . which would render all her plans for Nettle to be naught.

There was, however, one notable incident during that time. One night, I was cleaning the house before bed when Poppy came up to me. I had thought she was asleep like her mother and sister, so I jumped in surprise when she said my name.

"Rapunzel?"

"Y-yes, Poppy?" I said, still a little shaken.

"I—umm, my mother has hidden a journal written by your father. When I found it, I wanted to bring you the whole thing, but I knew she would notice. So instead, I . . . well, I've been skimming through it, and I found a page I thought you'd like to see."

She held out the ripped page of the journal, and I took it from her.

"I'll try to get you the whole journal one day, but I thought you needed to see this now."

"Thank you, Poppy," I said gratefully. It seemed a little strange that she had waited to tell me about it, but on further thought, I realized she probably felt guilty because it had taken so long for her to tell me of the letter her mother had forged.

She nodded somewhat awkwardly, and then she left to go to her and Nettle's room.

I immediately glanced down at the journal entry.

The most remarkable thing happened today. My wife and I were so distraught at not being able to have a child that we finally agreed to attempt to get our hands on some rapunzel. Unfortunately, the only place we knew the rare lettuce grew was the queen's garden. It was supposed to have many different types of plants, so we felt it was our only hope.

Hawthorn help me, I didn't want to be a thief. But we were desperate. So we went to the castle in the dead of night, and my wife waited outside as I went and filled a basket with fresh rapunzel. As I was leaving, however, the queen came across me. I begged her not to punish me and told her of my plight. I thought for certain I was to be taken to prison.

Instead, she had me bring my wife before her. After looking at us both, she said, "I can tell you are both good people who are sick at heart due to your childlessness. Because of that, I will give you a child that has been placed in my safekeeping. I have one condition, however."

"Anything! Anything!" my wife and I had cried.

"You must always honor any bargain made with a magical creature."

We couldn't do anything but agree. And when she brought us a beautiful baby girl, there were tears in our eyes, and we named her Rapunzel in honor of the lettuce that had led us to her.

I stared down at the torn page. I was glad Poppy had left, as I didn't know what I would have said to her. The journal entry explained why my mother had named me "Rapunzel," but more importantly, it explained why my father had been so keen on honoring deals made with a talking wolf, though his guilt was so great that it drove him to his death.

Who was my real mother? Why had she sent me to Queen Rose for safekeeping? Why had they thought rapunzel would help them have a child? Why had Queen Rose not wanted to keep me herself? I felt like I had more questions than ever.

Still, I was glad to have a piece of my father that I could take with me, and when Thorny finally returned, I felt as if I were in even better spirits.

To Iris's dismay, Thorny only gave her a three-hour dinner notice. She then proceeded to bark orders at me regarding how I needed to prepare the best meal I had ever made.

I had hated taking the coins Thorny gave me for food, but it was necessary for us to survive since Iris was loath to part with any of the fine things from Silverthorn that Thorny had given us. But even with such a cash flow, it was hard for me to justify spending ridiculous amounts on food; my gut instinct was to remain frugal. So while I planned a meal that was nicer than normal, I didn't cook the lavish dinner that Iris expected. I figured I wouldn't be there the next day to be admonished, and I didn't want my stepsisters to be punished for Iris's poor money-handling skills any more than they already would be.

But when I returned home with food from the market, I found Thorny outside waiting to speak to me.

"What are you doing here?" I whispered furiously as I pulled him into the barn, still hanging on to my basket of food.

He was unaffected by my upset. "I've got the supplies and maps waiting at the inn—didn't want your stepmother to accidentally see them—but I wanted to show you a few thi—"

"Is that a sword?" I interrupted, staring down at his side. I had thought he knew better than to bring one of those here by now.

"Yes, it is," he said with a grin, unsheathing the blade and holding it up for my inspection. "It's a new one."

I pushed the hand holding the sword away. "Thorny, you can't bring that with us. We have to be inconspicuous if we don't want to be the target of every bandit from here to the edge of Airland! And your clothes are way too flashy."

His face fell. "I thought I looked debonair."

"You're supposed to look downtrodden," I said, exasperated. "You need to go sell those clothes for some that look more beat-up."

"I'm not getting rid of the boots."

"Fine. Keep the boots. But everything else has to go, including the sword."

"I'm not selling the sword," he said stubbornly. "It's a beautiful antique."

"All right. We'll bury it, and you can come back for it later."

"Fine," he grumbled. The fact that he didn't argue over burying the sword made me think he realized my stepmother would probably take it if she found it lying around. "Can I bring a gun?"

"No!"

He sighed. "Fine."

I heard something jingle, and I looked over to see an unfamiliar horse standing in the barn. "What is that?" I said without thinking.

Thorny perked up. "That's my new mount. He's a Landdish Buckskin Dun."

I hadn't heard of that sort of horse before, and I examined him as best as I could. He was a sort of golden tan, with a black face and legs. I couldn't see his tail, but his black mane was streaked with gold. "He's very pretty."

"Handsome, you mean," Thorny corrected.

"Whatever. Anyway, you also need to get some worn tack—"

"Elle—"

"Don't you 'Elle' me. I'm serious, Thorny. We don't want people to look at us twice. And that horse's saddle just screams 'wealth.'"

"All right, Your Highness, all right," he said.

"These bandits aren't something to mess around with, Thorny."

"I get it. I just wanted to quest in style."

"You can quest in style on your own time. If this is my journey, I want to be in charge." I stared at him without blinking. This was the first opportunity I had ever been given to truly take control of my life, and I intended to make the most of it.

He looked away. "You're right. I'll go make some exchanges."

"Good. Now, leave your sword here, and I'll bury it for you." I had something else I needed to bury as well. I had been hiding the rose that had imprisoned me at Silverthorn in the barn. But since I was leaving this life behind, I didn't want to take it with me. Still, it felt wrong to burn the rose, so I intended to give it a proper burial. When Thorny returned for his sword, he could either take the flower as a last memento of me or leave it behind for good. I hoped he chose the latter.

"Go, Thorny," I told him, seeing him hesitate. "I'll talk to you later."

Muttering, he led his horse out of the barn and then mounted it and rode off.

Knowing I didn't have much time, I set aside my basket of food and pulled out a small box containing the rose from a pile of hay (*Like searching for a thorn in a haystack*, I thought wryly). I couldn't resist opening the box briefly to look at the rose. It had never regained that beautiful scarlet color it had retained at Silverthorn; instead, it remained a withered purplish brown. But I didn't see it as ugly, and it was hard to let the flower go. Though the rose was part of the reason my father was dead, I couldn't fault it. It had also helped me make a friend in Thorny, and that was something I could never regret.

I emptied a long wooden box containing some farming tools and then found one of Luna's old saddle blankets. Wrapping Thorny's sword tightly in the cloth, I put it inside the long box and then set the rose-box on top of it. I closed the big box with a sad sense of finality, wishing things could have been different.

I went outside the barn, where I dug a hole beside an old crate. When the hole was big enough, I lowered the box into it. After wiping something out of my eye, I used my hands to fill the hole with dirt and told myself I was returning the rose to the soil, where it belonged.

Still, later, as I prepared dinner with my stepmother hovering over me, my thoughts kept returning to that rose. Despite being uprooted from the soil, it hadn't died until taken away from the magic of Silverthorn. Wasn't that the key to making things blossom— keeping it in the ideal environment?

Though I knew how important this meal was to help me keep up my strength for the journey ahead, it was hard to make myself eat when dinner began. Mostly, I watched as Iris and Nettle made fools of themselves, with Poppy inserting occasional off-topic comments and Thorny's face turning into a thunderhead.

Miserable as I had been, I would miss them. They were family, after all, and I did care for them. Would they be able to survive without a more careful hand to guide them? With my father gone, I had stepped into that role as best as I could, but who would do it when I left?

Iris's voice broke through my thoughts: "I am so sorry for our poor fare, Your Highness. This must be nothing at all like the lavish meals to which you are accustomed. Of course, there is only so much one can do with a poor cook."

"I think it's delicious," Thorny said obstinately, and I gave him a grateful look.

Iris then began to extol the virtues of meals she had eaten as a young woman, and I stopped paying attention to her. Thorny caught my eye and made a "blah blah" motion with his hand, and I gave him a sharp shake of my head. He rolled his eyes but stopped the hand movement, and I hid a grin. Though Thorny was often moody, he did know how to make me smile.

The meal continued in an unremarkable fashion, except for an odd moment when Iris began laughing to herself for no obvious reason, and when it was all finally over, Thorny and I went out to the barn, where he had already stashed our supplies. Since Iris and my stepsisters rarely worked after dinner, I tried not to worry that they would stumble across the evidence of his preparations.

"I didn't sell my flashy outfit because I wanted to wear it to dinner—I didn't want to raise any suspicions," he explained when he caught me eyeing his immaculate appearance. "But I've got some clothes to change into."

I nodded. "We can't leave until everyone has gone to bed. Then I'll come out here to meet you. You'll need to wait a little while."

"Yeah, I figured that. I wanted to tell you—while I did find some maps of Airland, they're a little outdated, so we'll need to keep an eye out for some newer ones. Maybe once we actually get to Airland, we'll have better luck. I also found this amazing compass . . . ."

I let him ramble on. I knew we wouldn't need the maps since I intended to part with him once we entered Airland, and that knowledge was starting to make me feel guilty. With him being this excited about our "quest," could I really drop him the moment it was convenient for me? Or did I owe it to him to see it through, though I knew my journey wouldn't be ending with me as queen?

I looked over at Thorny's horse, which was staring at me intently with its dark eyes. As I reached out to touch his nose, I got the sense that Thorny truly had chosen a dependable mount, even if he had gone a bit overboard in setting up other parts of the journey. "What did you name your horse, Thorny?"

He looked perturbed at having been interrupted, but he answered: "Phoenix."

I raised an eyebrow. "A Landdish name?" I half-wondered if he had chosen the name out of spite toward my stepmother.

"I thought it fit since we're going to Airland. That *is* where his breed originates."

"He looks more like a Flint to me," I said, rubbing the horse's forehead.

"What—no French name?"

"I use French names for female animals. I like stone names for males."

He shook his head. "Whatever. Anyway, you're going to be reborn from the ashes like the legendary bird. So, in a sense, I'm naming Phoenix after you."

I couldn't help but smile to myself. "Thorny."

"What?" he said defensively.

My eyes fell on his cleanly shaven cheek, and I felt a strong urge to give it a light peck of gratitude. But I suppressed the impulse and said, "I'm going back to the house. But I'll meet you here around midnight, all right?" That should be enough time to ensure Iris was in a deep sleep.

"All right," Thorny said.

I turned toward the barn door and thought I saw a flash of movement. But I quickly dismissed it. I was on edge because of what was before me, and I could hardly be blamed for seeing things.

When I went inside the house, my stepmother berated me on the quality of the meal I had prepared, with Nettle throwing in some nasty comments of her own. I didn't argue with Iris when she said that cooked apples with cinnamon and sugar and butter were a bad idea for a dessert; I didn't cry when she said she had eaten better salads prepared by an old cook was who half-blind and one-handed. I simply listened to her litany of complaints until she released me to clean.

As I scrubbed the fireplace, I heard Nettle say: "What would His Highness think if he saw Cinderbella right now?"

Low though I was, I didn't burst into tears. I concentrated on minutiae instead. *I'll never have to clean this stone again,* I thought. *I won't mash my knees on that corner anymore.*

After completing various household tasks, I finished with the dishes. I did that a lot because it was a way for me to get some of the dirt off my hands. I also liked to use it as an opportunity to clean my face.

Once I finally made my way to bed, I was so exhausted it was hard to keep my eyes open. I actually dozed off once for a few minutes before startling myself awake. I looked at the clock on the mantle, glad that I still had time before I needed to go to Thorny, and then I reconsidered my side of the supply list.

I should have asked Thorny to buy me a few plain dresses. I had been wearing the black one Poppy had given me the whole time I had been home, and it was falling apart due to the vigorousness of my work. Not that I could have worn the dress even if it had been in pristine condition—a girl who was traveling in mourning clothes was certain to raise a few eyebrows.

Fortunately, I had found an old dress of mine the other day in a trunk which would fit somewhat, though it was too short. I had been hunting for clothes I could turn into rags or handkerchiefs, but that was one I felt was not ready to be scrapped yet. It wouldn't look very flattering on me, but that didn't matter. I needed to be beneath notice.

A few minutes later, I hastily changed into the dress and grabbed a bag I had packed with a few necessities in it. I glanced around the room and then on impulse wrote on a scrap of paper: *Goodbye.* It felt kind of cold, but I didn't know what else to say. In truth, it felt like my stepmother didn't even deserve that.

After placing the piece of paper on the mantle beside the clock, I left the house quietly and went out to the barn. What I found there wasn't what I expected.

Thorny's horse had a rider, but it wasn't him. Instead, Thorny was on the ground, gritting his teeth and telling said rider in a furious whisper, "*I told you,*

'*GET DOWN!*'"

"Poppy?" I rasped. What was she doing here?

My stepsister looked at me with defiance flaring in her eyes. "I heard you talking about going to Airland, and I want to come with you."

"Poppy—" I began, but she cut me off.

"If you make me stay," she said, "I'll run and tell Mother what you're doing."

"What are we, eight?" Thorny muttered to himself. Then, loudly, he said: "We aren't criminals." Still, he looked uneasy.

I knew how he felt. There was no telling what kind of trouble Iris could cause us.

"It may be dangerous," I said. Poppy was afraid of her own shadow, and I was hoping to dissuade her through logic.

"I don't care," she said stubbornly. Then she softened and gave me an entreating look. "Please, Labelle?"

The use of my old name notwithstanding, I could tell this meant a lot to Poppy. While her mother was a million times nicer to her than she was to me, Poppy was still often neglected or pushed aside in favor of Nettle. And while Nettle did pay some attention to Poppy, that attention only extended to allowing Poppy to act as her shadow. Could Poppy be blamed for wanting to escape Nettle and Iris?

Thorny's thoughts were not as charitable as mine. "No, no, no, *no!*" he exclaimed.

"You can come," I said suddenly.

"What?" Thorny squawked.

"As long as you call me 'Elle,'" I told her. Thorny squinted at me, and I advised him, "We could use another person for safety. And this is *my* journey, remember?"

"It's a deal, Elle," Poppy said quickly, obviously not wanting me to change my mind.

The prince crossed his arms. "Fine. But she's not riding on my horse. And I want you to know—I think this is a bad idea."

"She can share Luna with me," I said. "And it will be fine."

"She's gonna slow us down," he grumbled. But he grabbed Phoenix's reins and said to Poppy: "You win. Now, get down."

Poppy dismounted and moved to stand by me as Thorny led Phoenix out of the barn, cursing under his breath.

"Thanks, Elle," Poppy said. It was a genuine expression of gratitude, and it made me smile.

"You're welcome," I told her. She really was a good person when she wasn't with her mother or Nettle.

Poppy and I got Luna ready, and then we led her out of the barn. Thorny was standing beside Phoenix and holding a small book. As Poppy climbed up on my horse, Thorny gestured me over, and I walked to him.

"Here," he said, handing me the book. The cover read, *On Fairies.* "My mom gave it to me and said we might want to take a look at the marked passages. I've already read the whole thing, so I thought you might like to look at it. I know your stepmother was working you so hard you couldn't even stop to read a sign, but I think you might have a little time now." He looked down awkwardly at his hands. "I think you'll enjoy it, and it might help explain a little about . . . about why my mother is the way she is."

I smiled at him, shaking my head. Even now—when we were going on an "adventure"—he was encouraging me to read. "Thanks, Thorny. I'll give it back when I'm done."

He nodded and turned toward Phoenix, and I went back to Luna and Poppy, book in hand. Even though I was about to start a new life, I couldn't help but be a little curious about Thorny's mother. She was a true mystery to me. I certainly wouldn't mind to learn more about her and her kind.

CHAPTER 7:
THE TWELVE LANDED MARINERS

We didn't travel very far that night; we just went into the Devil Beast's Woods. It was actually in the opposite direction from where we were headed, but the idea was to quickly go to a place where my stepmother wouldn't find us. Poppy said she left a letter saying she had run off with a boy, but I didn't believe her. She valued her mother's opinion too much to give her such a story. But I didn't press for the truth.

We set up camp on the forest floor. Thorny only bought two pallets to take with us, but Poppy had evidently had enough notice of our plans that she had come prepared with bedding of her own. She was also in a well-used dress rather than a black or lavender one, so that was one less thing for the prince to gripe about.

Thorny showed us how to make a fire to ward off the chill of the night, and for some reason, that made me smile. Perhaps it was because it was hard for him to remember to be angry when he was giving instructions on the right way to have an adventure.

As I looked at him over the flicker of the campfire and listened to him give an intent Poppy tips on how to best skewer "small prey" (he refused to say "rabbit" for my sake, but I knew that was what he meant), I thought of how boyish he looked. Maybe it was because he still viewed the world with a somewhat childish mindset in spite of—or perhaps, paradoxically, because of—what the world had thrown at him. I wanted to wipe that hair out of his eyes. He had trimmed it since we left Silverthorn, but his bangs were still too long.

I found my eyes drawn to his mouth and thought of how that smile of his always seemed to be all-or-nothing. He wasn't good at pretending to feel what he didn't, as evidenced by his multitude of proposals to me. In many ways, he was an open book for the world to read. I hadn't really understood that before. When he was a wolf, he had seemed like a walking contradiction, and his motives had been hard for me to gauge. But now that I knew the reason a wolf could know how to read books and recite plays, everything made more sense.

He saw me staring at him and smiled. He gave a little nod of his head to acknowledge my gaze, and I looked away. The fire suddenly felt too hot, and I backed away from it.

Remembering the book Thorny was letting me borrow, I went and fetched it. My body was too filled with adrenaline to let me sleep yet, so I decided to read.

I flipped through the pages to find the marked passages Thorny had mentioned. The beginning of the book looked like it was about sorcerers, which the author claimed would also be of interest to anyone wanting to learn more about fairies. I found the first flagged section, and it said:

Every sorcerer has a soul-brother. This refers to a wild animal, such as a hawk or boar, that a sorcerer is connected with spiritually. Usually, a soul-brother will first appear during a time of crisis, though this is not always the case.

I wondered if the same might hold true for fairies, but I hadn't seen any animals following Queen Rose around, so I wasn't sure. What was significant about this passage then?

I sighed, knowing I should go to bed soon, but I couldn't help flipping through the pages to find another marked passage. The next one I found had a header called "Curses."

Fairies have different abilities, but most can perform several different kinds of spells. Most spells fall under the categories of earth, water, fire, wind, and lightning. One category that all fairies have some measure of skill in is spirit.

One of the strongest spirit spells is a curse. There are two basic types of curses. The first kind is called a "benediction." In the case of a benediction, a good fairy ultimately wishes to help someone. This might be accomplished, for instance, by turning a spoiled young man into a toad. While people other than the intended target may be negatively affected, the ultimate goal of a benediction is to help all who are brought under its influence, whether through promotion of love or positive character traits. However, such a goal may be subverted by the actions of those affected by the benediction. Often, the key to breaking this kind of curse is to prove one's worth or to allow the power of love to work its magic.

I had to stop reading for a moment. I knew what Queen Rose had done was a benediction. Considering what had happened to my father, it didn't feel that way, yet I knew Queen Rose's intentions had been good.

My eyes fell back on the text, and I read the rest of the section.

In a malediction, there is no good will to be found. The intent of this spell is not to teach a lesson, but to destroy. Only a desperate fairy resorts to such measures, for a malediction requires sacrifice to be effective. They say no curse is unbreakable, however. Love—particularly romantic love—is especially useful at undoing curses.

It is to be noted that it is much more difficult to curse another magic user, which is why battles between fairies and sorcerers have been known to be so bloody.

The section ended there, and though I would have liked to know more, it didn't seem to matter that much. I wasn't facing a malediction. And hopefully, Thorny's mother would never resort to such a desperate measure.

My eyes heavy, I packed the book up. I was going to need my rest, and it was silly to delve back into the world of books when I was about to enter a life where I would have no time for them.

"I'm going to bed," I announced to Thorny and Poppy.

Thorny looked up and smiled at me, and for some

reason, my pulse quickened. "Good night, Elle," he told me. "Sweet dreams."

I nodded at Poppy, who inclined her head in return, and then I went and curled up on my pallet. Though it wasn't terribly comfortable, I wore my dress to bed. I tried not to think about how Thorny—when he was a wolf—had already seen me stripped down to my shift.

After I fell asleep, I dreamed I was knee-deep in roses and surrounded by mirrors. Each mirror held an enthusiastic Thorny talking about the great adventures we had in store. But there was something off about it, like his excitement was feigned.

Upon waking in the morning, I found myself looking at him warily to see whether he was going to start rambling about our upcoming adventures, but he just suggested we hurry and leave New Fountain far behind before Iris sent men with torches and pitchforks after us (which really didn't make sense with it being a bright morning, but I didn't tell him that). There were dark circles under his eyes, like he hadn't slept well, and I thought of asking him about it, but something on his face suggested it would be better not to.

We made good time, and though I feared we would see someone who would try to stop us and drag me back to my stepmother's house, we made it past New Fountain without any trouble. There was a heart-stopping point when I thought I saw a flash of red through the trees, but I dismissed it as a fleeing wild animal and brought my mind back to the journey.

The real trouble arose after we entered a wooded area not far outside the village. We were walking down the road through the forest when twelve men in masks appeared from the trees and surrounded us.

Poppy clenched me so tightly it was hard to breathe, but Thorny simply appeared disgusted and said: "Bandits. Seriously?"

"We're not bandits," a man with a long mustache corrected. "We're highwaymen."

Thorny pulled out a dagger and pointed it at the mustached man, but the bandits merely laughed at him.

"Oh, no," said a mountain of a man in mock-fear. "The mighty boy is going to poke us with his tiny stick." That set off another round of guffaws.

Thorny's face was scarlet now, and he threw a glare my way. "I *would* come at you with my sword, but *she* made me leave it at home."

"Awww," said Mountain, "trouble with the missus already?"

"She's not my wife," grumbled Thorny. Somehow, his face had turned redder.

"No?" spoke up Mustache. He walked over and traced a finger down my leg. I kicked his hand away, holding tightly to Luna's reins, and he laughed. "Then perhaps you wouldn't mind if I made her *my* missus?"

In the blink of an eye, Thorny had leaped off his horse and pinned the man to the ground, dagger against his throat. "You lay another finger on her," he growled, "and I'll take the whole hand."

Poppy shrieked, and all I could think was *wolf*.

The other bandits moved forward with weapons

brandished, ready to skewer the prince. One man was even pointing a gun at Thorny. I cast my eyes around for a weapon, but even if I could find something, I would never reach Thorny in time.

Fortunately, the bloodshed that seemed inevitable did not occur. There was one bandit with a clear head, and he called out: "Wait!"

The crowd parted to let him through, and I got a good look at him. He was a tall and slender man whose mask made him look mysterious rather than sinister. But perhaps that was helped by the fact that he had a stylish captain's hat perched on his head.

"Can't you see this is a man in love? Come on, boy. Stand up."

Though Thorny looked disgruntled at having been called a "boy," he must have realized the danger he was in, as he slowly pulled the dagger away from Mustache's throat and rose to his feet. A pair of bandits stepped forward to help the man up, and he glared at Thorny.

Meanwhile, the bandit in a captain's hat held his hand out for Thorny's dagger. The disguised prince took a quick look around, as if to gauge whether he could take on all of them, before he relinquished the weapon.

"Thank you, boy. It really *is* for the best. I am Captain Crestwood, and this is my crew." He made an elegant sweep of his hand. "We are a band of heart-brothers, and we call ourselves the Twelve Landed Mariners."

"Were you pirates?" blurted Thorny.

The captain shook his head and gave a dramatic sigh. "No. We were men on a ship that saw some terrible sights at sea, and we barely made it back alive. We swore then that we would never return to those briny waters. But who has use for seamen on land? So we have been forced to turn to petty thievery to buy our bread."

I doubted it was as romantic as he made it sound, but Thorny looked convinced.

"What could you possibly want from us poor travelers?" I asked, trying to act meek and sweet.

"Ah," said the captain, tilting his head with a smile. "What is your name, miss?"

Despite my misgivings, I let him take my hand and kiss it. However, I quickly snagged it back when I saw the murderous look on Thorny's face. I didn't want to encourage the prince to cause us *more* trouble.

"Rapunzel Beauregard," I answered him. It was only after speaking that I realized perhaps I should have given him a fake name.

"Well, Miss Beauregard," began Captain Crestwood, "you would indeed fit perfectly the picture of worn travelers were it not for your young man's horse."

I glanced at Phoenix and then turned my eyes back to the bandit leader, a sinking feeling in my gut. "What do you mean?"

"There are many who would never realize what a prize horse that is. However, I, in spite of my years at sea, have a good—dare I say 'excellent'?—eye for horseflesh, and I recognized that coveted breed the moment I saw it. I knew then there was more to you than meets the eye."

I was so angry it was a wonder that steam wasn't coming out of my ears. No wonder I had never seen a horse like this one before. I turned the full force of my fury on Thorny. "You brought . . . a *rare horse* . . . in *spite of everything I said?*"

He shrugged, unconcerned. "I needed a good mount for the journey. Landdish Buckskin Duns are known for their endurance."

"Much though I hate to interrupt this lovers' quarrel," said the captain, "I'm afraid we must abscond with your valuables and be off. Yewan, Crane—if you would be so kind as to assist the ladies off their horse."

Two men stepped forward, and I said in a panic, "What?"

Captain Crestwood raised an eyebrow. "Did you believe I would allow you to keep your beast of burden? Come, now—even a Magnolian horse will fetch a nice price if you can find the right buyer."

As Yewan and Crane manhandled me and a shrieking Poppy off Luna, I recalled how I once was willing to do anything to keep my horse—including taking a wolf on as a companion. Was there something I could do this time?

"Please," I begged as I was dumped on the ground. "You can take whatever you want, but leave me my horse!"

"And those maps!" Thorny cried out. "Come on, take the coins, but don't take the maps!" He was watching helplessly as a man dug through Phoenix's saddlebags, curious as to whether there was much of interest. The bandit acted as if he had all the time in the world.

"Sorry," the mountain of a man told Thorny. "But those are valuable, too."

"Hey!" Thorny shouted again, looking at a different

bandit, who was rifling through Luna's saddlebags and tossing things of no value to the ground. "That book on fairies was a gift from my mother!"

But nothing we said could convince robbers not to rob, and as they prepared to leave with most of our belongings, Mustache turned to Thorny and jeered: "You're lucky we make it a policy to leave people's shoes alone. You have some fine buckles."

The captain tipped his hat in farewell, and then they were gone.

Thorny and I stared after them; Poppy stood quietly behind us, as if our forms would serve as a barrier between the bandits and her.

Though we had needed Thorny's money for food, I wasn't too upset about that loss since I had fortunately had the foresight to hide a few coins away. What *did* upset me was the fact that my association with Thorny had nearly cost me Luna once before . . . and might have torn her from me entirely this time.

Wanting to strangle someone, I swiveled toward Poppy. My face must have looked fierce, as she took a step backward.

"Poppy," I gritted, "tell your flashy friend that I intend to get my horse back, *with or without* his assistance."

Poppy looked to Thorny helplessly. But he was annoyed, too.

"'Flashy friend'?" he said. "I'll have you know that if someone hadn't made me bury my pixie-bit *sword*, I could have taken down all those bandits, and we wouldn't be in this mess!"

"Poppy," I said, trying to rein in my temper without much success, "tell your fat-headed companion that if egos could squash bandits, then we would've made pancakes out of all of them. But since they *can't*, he'd better be glad he only had a dagger—because they probably would have impaled him otherwise."

Thorny was red-faced now. "Poppy, tell your higher-than-thou stepsister that I have practiced swordplay with some of Magnolia's greatest instructors, and I know just how to stick it—"

"Poppy," I cut in loudly, "tell your arrogant sword-wielding *pal* that I know exactly where he can stick it, and he can start by—"

"Enough!" Poppy cried. "You're fighting like cougars and wolves, and it's ridiculous. Now, Elle, let's think this through. Trying to get back the horses and everything else is suicide. We should continue without them."

"No," I said stubbornly. "I'm getting Luna back."

"And I'm getting back my maps," Thorny added. "And my book. And my dagger—"

"The main problem is figuring out where the bandits live," I told Poppy. "You and I would be recognized in the village. Can you tell your royal *friend* he needs to go to the pub and ask around?"

"Oh, sure," Thorny muttered. "Make *me* do all the work. That's just like a woman."

Poppy sighed. "There's no need."

"What do you mean?" I asked.

"Nettle and I visited the pub a lot. For me, it started with checking on your father, and then it became more about . . . well, seeing the men. And men with alcohol in them like to talk. I can take you to the bandits' house, but it's a bad idea. They say no one ever goes there and comes back."

"Well, someone had to go there to be able to tell that story," I said. "So lead the way."

Poppy looked at the ground. "Fine. But it can be a bit of a journey on foot—I think they often camp in the woods when they have small plunder. We should take the road a little ways before going off it. It's not like we have anything worth stealing now anyway."

"I do have a few coins in my shoe," I admitted, "but I think you're right."

We gathered the few items that the bandits had left us and got on the road and began to walk. After perhaps five minutes, Thorny complained, "I'm hungry. We should go back to the village and buy some more food. After all, I can't even set up a snare for a rabbit seeing as I *have no dagger to skin it with.*"

I pinched my lips together. "We're not using my coins unless there's an emergency. And we're going to ration what little food we have left." The bandits had taken the tastier food items and left us with the less desirable stuff like dried meat. I had the feeling that if Poppy and I had been male, they would have taken even that.

And then, to make matters worse, a cranky man with a horse and cart appeared on the road. In itself, that wasn't terrible, but I was hungry, too, and the aroma emanating from the cart was heavenly. I could especially pick out the scent of apple pie. It didn't take much of my imagination to picture myself holding a piece in my hands and biting through the crisp crust to the warm inside—I would then roll the soft apple bits in my mouth and simply savor their sweetness, and it would slide down my throat oh so warmly . . .

I swallowed, pushing the daydream away. We

couldn't afford to spend money on dessert.

But Thorny's thoughts must have paralleled my initial ones, as he said hopefully, "Is that pie?" If he had been a wolf, his nostrils would have been quivering.

The man stopped his horse since we were in his way, and Thorny practically cantered up to him.

"Come on, you *have* to let me have a sample of your wares," the prince said, his voice a plea.

The pieman looked him over skeptically, eyeing the impoverished look I had forced upon Thorny, and then he said, "Show me your Oaks first."

Thorny reached automatically for his coin-purse, only to realize the bandits had taken it from him. He colored and said, "Umm, I don't have any."

The man's tanned face darkened. "And I don't have anything you can try if you can't buy."

Thorny stood straighter, taking on a regal air. "Don't you know who I am?"

The surly man lifted an eyebrow, unimpressed.

Thorny looked at me, and I could see that the position he was in had begun to dawn on him. Even if he *did* claim to be a prince, there was no way this pie-seller would believe him. "Umm, come on, Elle. Show him your money."

"No, Thorny," I said calmly, stepping off the road. "Now let the poor man through."

He moved with great reluctance, as did Poppy, and we all three watched as the pieman drove off. My stomach gave me an angry reminder of how hungry I was. Though I was trying to do the smart thing, I felt disappointed, too.

Thorny was just as vocal as my belly. "I can't

believe you let an opportunity like that escape us. What are the odds of meeting a pieman here anyway?"

"We have to guard our Oaks until we get more," I told him. "We don't know when that will be."

"Well, my stomach might eat me before I get there," Thorny complained. "I have the appetite of a wolf."

I rolled my eyes and started walking.

Though she spoke quietly, I could hear Poppy telling Thorny, "Surely, it couldn't have hurt for us each to have one piece."

I sighed and tried to think of other things. I didn't know why *I* had to be the bad guy.

CHAPTER 8:

OF HUNGER AND BANDITS

I t was hard to ignore my hunger pangs because Thorny continued to complain about his stomach loudly and constantly. The incident with the pieman certainly didn't help quell his hunger pangs.

When we came to the small cabin visible from the road that Poppy said marked where we needed to step into the woods, Thorny saw a nanny goat standing in a small pen near it.

"Great Gawain!" he exclaimed. "Isn't that lucky? I've got this."

Puzzled, Poppy and I followed him over to the goat to see what he was talking about.

"Don't worry," he tried to assure us. "I read about this in a book. You want a beautiful spread? Watch this." Then he turned to address the goat. "Little goat, if you are able, pray deck out my table."

We waited in silence.

"Is something supposed to happen?" Poppy asked at last.

Thorny turned and glared at her. "Yes. Maybe I didn't say it right. Nanny goat, if you're able, please deck out my table." He waited, but nothing happened.

I shook my head in exasperation. "Maybe you're supposed to provide food *and* a table, and then the goat eats them both. Come on, Thorny, this isn't one of your books. The real world doesn't work like that. But you *were* right that we're lucky—we can get some milk from the goat. That might help our stomachs."

Though Thorny was in a pout because of his failure to provide us with a magnificent table of food, he, too, took his hand at filling a canteen with milk. We were fortunate that an angry occupant didn't exit the cabin to stop us. Considering our luck thus far, I wouldn't have been surprised if it had happened.

We had to make do with milk and beef jerky for our dinner that night, and when we woke in the morning, we were all ravenous. But amid Thorny's complaints, we started up again, and while Poppy's directions to the bandits got a little hazy, I said, "I have a hunch about where to go." I wasn't sure where it had come from, but I had a gut feeling about it.

I half expected Thorny to argue about my chosen path, but he simply frowned thoughtfully and said nothing.

As I led us forward, I heard a strange sound in the bushes behind us, and I turned to see what it was. I saw a streak of reddish brown, and I froze.

"Is someone there?" I called out, though not too loudly.

Thorny frowned at me. "Who are you talking to?"

"I . . . I thought I saw someone." I remembered another time I had seen a streak of color. Could someone be following us? It wasn't one of the bandits, was it?

"I didn't see anything," Poppy volunteered.

"Yeah, neither did I," said Thorny. "Maybe it was just a deer or something."

"Yeah, maybe," I murmured, but I wasn't so sure. Taking in a deep breath, I began to lead us once more.

Before long, the bandits' cabin was looming before us, and we crouched behind some bushes and studied it. The building was fairly large since it was meant to hold twelve men, and I was surprised few people had ever come across it. Beside it was something that wasn't a stable so much as six poles with a roof over them, and tied to those poles were five horses, two of which I recognized.

"Guys," Poppy whispered, "I really think this is a bad idea."

"I'm getting Luna," I said. "It's non-negotiable. We just have to figure out the best way to do it. I think we should jump on the horses and run."

"But the big bad highwaymen may not like that," said a voice from behind me.

"Well, of course they—" I began, only to freeze as I realized that it wasn't Thorny speaking. Slowly, the three of us turned to face Mustache and Mountain.

"I say we skin them," said Mustache, looking at us darkly as he ran a hand along the edge of his sword.

Mountain shook his head. "The cap'n wouldn't like

that. You know he likes to make these decisions."

"They're lucky," said Mustache with a sneer.

Somehow, we didn't feel so lucky. Especially not when the two bandits bound our hands behind our backs and practically shoved us into the cabin.

"Watch it," Thorny said sharply as Mustache actually did push me.

Mustache gave him a nasty grin and grabbed the back of my arm. I shook him off and gave him a sour look of my own.

"Cap'n," said Mountain once we were all inside, "look what the cat drug in."

Captain Crestwood had been laughing with a few of his band, but he quickly sobered upon seeing us. He shook his head and said in a disappointed tone, "I had hoped that was the last we'd see of you, entertaining though you were. Now that you have found our hideout, I must decide what to do with you, and I'm afraid it won't be pleasant."

Thorny and I looked at each other, our minds working furiously, and then I blurted, "We could be your servants!"

Thorny, ever the storyteller, ran with it. "We could definitely do that! You see, we've been running away from a cruel master and hoping for a better life. We took money and horses and everything to try to escape to Airland. But by a stroke of luck, we ended up here. Look at this place." He made a big gesture to the contents of the cabin, which were in terrible disarray. "You could use some servants. Elle is a skilled cook, and Poppy is excellent at cleaning." Both Poppy and I glared at him, but he ignored us. "I have great muscles for lifting. Couldn't you use a few servants of your own to *really* live like kings?"

The faces of the bandits showed mixed feelings—some of them were thoughtful and some doubtful. But only one face really mattered.

"Great muscles, you say?" echoed the captain in mock-interest. Laughter filled the room at the implication. "Though you are but a pint of a boy, I may give you a chance to prove your usefulness."

"A pint?" Thorny repeated indignantly. "I'm at least a full gallon!"

Captain Crestwood chuckled. "Indeed, you *are* full of it."

Several bandits guffawed.

"I'll tell you what," said the bandit leader, "I happen to know there's a man who will be taking a cow to market. If you can steal that cow and return it here, we will let you all leave with the ladies' pretty little brown horse and a pouch of coins—"

"What about *my* horse?" Thorny cut in.

"I'm afraid your horse is worth much more to me than a cow, so we'll be holding on to him," said the captain. "But if you fail to steal the cow, we keep the girls and decide what to do with you." A man behind him slid a finger across his throat in an overly dramatic slicing motion.

"Thorny," I said loudly, trying to get his attention. Thorny was a prince, not a thief, and we could try to find a different way to get Luna back.

Thorny turned to me with a cocky grin and said: "I can do this, Elle. I read about it in a book once. There was this guy that sought shelter at a house of bandits. They had him prove himself by stealing an ox that a man was taking to market. I just have to do what he did."

"Thorny, real life is not like your books—"

"Come, lass," said the captain. "Your young man wants to prove himself."

"He's not *my* young man," I spluttered, "and I really don't think—"

"I'll do it," Thorny said.

"Then let's be off quickly," said the captain, eyeing him in ill-concealed amusement. "Men, tie the girls to a couple of chairs. Orris, you keep an eye on them. The rest of you, come with me to watch this boy's great plan unfold."

Poppy and I were bound to chairs as the captain had instructed, and then all the bandits save one filed out of the house.

Orris was short and thin, but he looked nice for a bandit, and I thought I could talk to him without fearing he would snap at me. One point in his favor was the fact that he was playing with a deck of cards instead of making threats.

"Is Captain Crestwood really going to . . . kill my friend?" I asked hesitatingly.

Orris looked up from the table. "Doubt it, miss. Not his way. But you've put us in a terrible bind."

"What do you mean?"

"Not much good to be a bandit if people don't fear you, now is it? Lettin' people leave our hideout—doesn't exactly fill anyone with fear, now, does it?"

"Are you g-going to k-kill the two of us?" Poppy asked. She was pale and looked like she might get sick. She really didn't have the courage for adventuring. Quite frankly, I was beginning to think I didn't either.

"Doubt it," Orris said. "Cap'n is a gentleman

through and through. Would cut off his own arm before he'd kill a lady, I reckon."

"A gentleman who steals from people?" I asked with raised brow.

"Yes'm. There's honor even among thieves."

I tilted my head. "The honorable thing would be to let us go."

"Aye, but there's your man to think about. Couple of scared girls who think they saw bandits? Easy to play off. But add him to the mix, and it could bring down hordes of villagers on our heads."

"That's not what we're after," I protested.

He leaned forward a bit. "And what *are* you all after?"

That depends on which one of us you ask, I thought. Out loud, I said, "I just want to go to Airland." That was the truth. I wasn't really trying to get the Arm of Avalon. That was Thorny's dream, not mine.

Orris gave me a sympathetic look, perhaps hearing the strain in my voice. I felt certain I could convince him to let Poppy and I go. But I wasn't going to abandon Thorny to these bandits, and a one-woman rescue team (for I knew Poppy wouldn't be much help) wasn't going to save Thorny's life. But from the inside, maybe I could actually figure out something. For now, there was nothing to do but wait.

And wait we did. At last, however, Thorny was brought in amid raucous laughter. His face was red, and when I gave him a questioning look, he gave a sideways jerk of his head. He hadn't stolen the cow. I wasn't sure whether to be relieved he wasn't made into a thief or scared he was going to die.

"Ho!" said Mountain. "You have quite the smart

fellow here!"

The bandits laughed harder.

"What happened?" I asked, speaking loudly so I could be heard above their guffaws.

"How about you tell the story to your lady love?" suggested the captain.

Thorny turned even redder. "It should've worked," he mumbled.

"Only in your books!" one bandit replied in obvious mirth.

When I looked to Thorny for an explanation, he said: "In the story, the young man put a shoe in the path of the man with the ox and then ran ahead and put another down."

"And then the cow-man is supposed to pass by the first shoe, only to leave his ox once he finds the second shoe and go back," said Mountain.

"And then I was supposed to steal the cow," grumbled Thorny.

"Only tell 'er what happened instead," said a different bandit.

"The man took his cow with him," Thorny said, gritting his teeth.

Mountain snickered. "So now your young man has no cow and no shoes!" That set the bandits off again.

I personally didn't see what was so funny, but I didn't intend to spoil their mood and make them feel murderous instead. I also didn't want to ask the question foremost in my head: *What do you intend to do with Thorny now?*

But the bandits' leader almost seemed to read my mind. "Your young man's a funny one," he said to me. "We haven't had this much fun in a while, ay, Burl?"

He was looking at the mountain of a man.

"Aye, cap'n. Not since we were sea-farers and I littered Valerian's bunk with cheese and watched the rats come to play." The bandits laughed, and a few slapped the back of a sour-looking man that must have been Valerian.

"Perhaps we won't off you quite so quickly, boy," said Captain Crestwood. "Tell me, do you know any jokes or riddles?"

Thorny cast his eyes around frantically as he tried to find some inspiration. "Uhhh, do you know the riddle about the man whose wife was turned into a flower? He was supposed to pick her out from two other identical flowers in the morning, though she was allowed to spend the night with him. So, how did he do it?"

"She was the only flower without dew on her," Captain Crestwood said. "Try a newer one."

Thorny pursed his lips and thrust his hand up into his hair at the back. He began a riddle haltingly:

"*When Dawn comes, I . . . out of an ivory prison . . . do— do break.*

Then up through . . . the afternoon, I with . . . fiery heat do, erm, bake.

But when cruel Eve arrives to . . . ah, strip away my plenty,

You can see with ease that . . . my—my stomach stands empty.

What am I?"

"A baker," Valerian said instantly. Perhaps he was trying to prove himself smart after his earlier embarrassment.

But Burl hit him in the head. "Not a baker, you nit!"

"That's a new one," the captain said. "Somewhat crude in its presentation, though, for a riddle that has been passed on. Did you make it up on the spot?"

I thought I saw a muscle in Thorny's cheek twitch. "Does it matter?" he asked.

The bandits' leader smiled. "No, I guess not. Please say it again."

Thorny gave the riddle again, though it sounded slightly different from the first time, and then Crestwood said to his men: "Any guesses?"

"A housewife!"

"A chicken!"

"A criminal."

"A bandit!"

The answers kept pouring in, and Thorny began looking more triumphant, until at last the captain held up a hand. "A dragon," he said.

Thorny lowered his head in defeat, utterly deflated. "Yeah."

Captain Crestwood smiled. "And now, a joke."

Thorny must have been waiting for that, as he responded quickly: "Why is a baby unicorn like a frog with a sore throat?" He paused for only a second. "Because they both know what it's like to be a little horse (hoarse)."

That produced a few snickers and a great many groans from the bandits. Captain Crestwood laughed and gave Thorny a slap on the back. "The good news, boy, is you'll live to jest another day. Tie him up, men. Orris, stand guard outside for a few minutes to give the boy some time to say a few personal things to these two young women. The rest of you scallywags, come with me to find some fresh booty."

Thorny was tied to a chair in front of me and Poppy, and then all the bandits filed out in a disorganized fashion. I looked at Thorny, filled with relief, and I wanted to say something nice, but all I could manage was: "You're lucky you aren't dead."

"It's not luck; it's wit," he retorted, but I thought he looked relieved in spite of his bravado.

"Can't you two stop fighting?" Poppy asked in a tight voice. "Aren't you scared we're all going to be killed?"

"Some things are stronger than fear," said Thorny. "Like hunger. It would have been nice if they'd fed us before they left. Maybe that Orris guy will give us something when he thinks we're done saying sweet nothings to each other."

"How did you ever survive as a wolf anyway?" I asked. "I'm surprised there are any chickens left at Silverthorn."

Poppy whimpered.

I ignored her. I was mad. But most of all, I was scared. What were they going to do to us? "You'd better hope they kill you when they get back, because if they don't, I might do the job for them. And I won't be nearly as gentle."

Thorny rolled his eyes, unaffected by my threat. "Well, our Silverthorn honeymoon sure ended when we left the castle grounds, didn't it?"

"The next person who even implies that I'm your woman is going to learn just—"

"Guys!" Poppy shrieked.

"What?" Thorny and I snapped.

"A rat!"

Thorny and I turned our gazes to the floor, and sure enough, a big fat rat was staring at us with dark beady eyes.

CHAPTER 9:

THE SMELL OF A RAT

I hate rats, I hate rats, I hate rats," Poppy was squeaking in some sort of high-pitched mantra under her breath.

"It won't hurt you," I told her, but she was too busy panicking to pay any attention to me.

The rat took a few steps closer to my stepsister and started grooming itself. She nearly had a conniption and squealed, "*Rat!*"

"I've got an idea," Thorny said loudly.

I turned a glare on him. "You need to start keeping those to yourself. They've brought us diddly squat so far."

"Hey, my ideas haven't turned out *that* badly!"

"Oh, please," I scoffed, "when have you had an

idea that went right?"

But that remark apparently hit him hard, and he didn't respond; he simply looked down at the ropes binding him.

An unexpected wave of guilt swept over me. I didn't need to be so mean. He was probably scared, too. "Thorny, I'm sorry I said that. Look—I'll listen to your idea."

He squinted at me suspiciously, but he evidently didn't want to look a gift pegasus in the mouth, as he said, "Girls tend to have a more special bond with animals, right?"

"So says the guy who was once turned into a wolf," I muttered, unable to help myself.

He narrowed his eyes but continued as though he hadn't heard me. "All you have to do is talk to the rat and ask it to chew through our bonds."

I raised both eyebrows. "That's one of the most ridiculous things I've ever heard. I hate to break it to you, Thorny, but this isn't some fairytale. You need to get your head out of your books. Goats don't sprout tables, and rats don't help humans."

"Elle," he said plaintively. He didn't say anything else—just that nickname he had given me.

Looking into those green eyes, I couldn't help but soften. He made think of a hurt puppy, and I wondered if he had always had that look in his repertoire or if he was just now trying it out on me.

"What?" I asked, but without any gruffness.

"You're good with animals, Elle, and if anyone can do this, it's you."

Ever since returning to New Fountain, I had been run ragged and sleep-deprived. Combine that with my sorrow over my father's death, and I was *really* on edge. It certainly hadn't helped that I had been forced to handle Iris's and Nettle's abuse without saying a word of complaint. Now, I was unjustly taking all that out on Thorny. But the only thing *he* wanted was to help me, and it wasn't right for me to treat him like that.

I took a deep breath to calm myself. "All right, Thorny. I'll try it."

This was stupid, and I didn't even know what Thorny expected me to do, so I simply gazed at the little creature and said half-heartedly, "Hey, rat, come here."

The rat looked at me.

"You need to put effort into it, Elle!" exclaimed Thorny. "You have to convince the rat that what you want is worth its time."

I nodded and stared at the creature. Gently, I said, "Hey, there. Come here, little fellow. I need your help. Can you come and chew off my bonds?"

The rat scratched its ear with a small pink hand, twitched its nose in contemplation, and then came scurrying forward.

Poppy, who wasn't exactly being quiet to begin with, let out a wail as the rat climbed up my leg and moved around to my back. "It's eating her hands off," she said with a whimper.

"Shut up," Thorny said sharply. His thoughts probably paralleled mine—one shriek from Poppy, and Orris would be here in an instant. That would end all chances of escape. "Just close your eyes and think of kittens and chicks and rabbit kits or something."

Though Poppy still wasn't quiet, her whimpers became more muted when she shut her eyes.

I had to fight the urge to squirm as the rat's naked tail tickled my hands. The rope holding me in place wasn't so thin that a rodent could chew through it instantly, and every second that ticked by made me fear I would find Orris at the door. But at last, the final strand broke, and I was able to remove my other bonds and rub my chafed wrists in relief.

The rat ran back down to the floor, and I said, "Thank you, little fellow."

He let out a squeak and then disappeared into a hole in the wall.

I turned to Thorny, who seemed a little stunned. "I didn't think it would be *that* easy," he said. Then he seemed to reevaluate his position and threw at me: "I told you so."

I shook my head and laughed, too relieved to be annoyed. It was beyond lucky that we might actually be getting out of this alive.

Poppy was muttering to herself and still had her eyes closed, so I freed her first. She seemed surprised to suddenly find her bonds gone and looked at me in confusion.

I allowed myself a brief instant to stretch cramped muscles. I was trying not to think about how hidden in that rat's squeak had been something that sounded a lot like "*sure*."

"Hey, what about me?" Thorny said indignantly.

I gave him a sweet smile. "I think maybe we ought to leave you and your 'rare horse' here with the bandits. You seemed pretty chummy to me."

"Oh, come on," he protested.

I chuckled to myself and decided to take pity on him. I began working on the ropes that held his hands first, trying to ignore the strange jolt that went through me every time I accidentally touched the warm skin of his hands. When I finished with that, I untied the ropes that bound him to the chair.

Finally, he was able to stand. As he did so, he glanced at the door—likely fearing Orris's return as much as I was—and then he moved forward to recover what the bandits had taken from him.

But after he had gotten what was rightfully ours, he started to take a few more things. When he put on new boots, I didn't intend to comment. When he grabbed a few updated maps, I bit my tongue. But when he grabbed a sword with a gem-encrusted scabbard, I protested, "*Thorny.*"

He turned a suffering look on me. "We have to protect ourselves, Elle. My dagger's good for skinning animals and not much else. Just be glad I don't intend to grab one of those guns."

I sighed. "Fine." I only hoped we weren't about to bring more trouble on our heads.

Then he turned to a giant chest. There was no lock on it, so all he had to do was squat and lift the heavy lid.

"I've never seen so many golden Oaks," Poppy said, peering over the prince's shoulder.

"I don't feel right about this," I said uneasily. "We should just count out the amount they took from us and go."

"All of this was unlawfully gained," Thorny pointed out. "They're going to use it for their own purposes anyway. We could use a few more coins for food."

I stared down at the pile and thought of how I could use a little extra money to start my life in

Airland. "All right," I conceded reluctantly. But I felt guilty about it.

Once our bags were full—their contents also including some of the bandits' food, which Thorny had insisted on taking as our due—there came the issue of what to do about Orris. I had begun to feel kindly toward him for giving us so much time alone together, though I knew he wouldn't be happy to learn we were about to escape.

"I can run my sword through him," volunteered Thorny.

I looked at him in horror. "Thorny, no! I don't care if he *is* a bandit. You don't go around *killing* people."

Thorny rolled his eyes. Muttering something about bleeding hearts, he went and picked up a club from a weapon rack. "Fine. I'll hit him over the head with this."

"Can you really sneak up on him?" Poppy asked.

"I'm used to hunting and being quiet," said Thorny with unwavering confidence.

I bit my lip. "But what if he sees you?"

"I'm a prince, remember?" he said, wiggling his eyebrows. "I know my way around a sword."

There was nothing for me to do but concede.

Carefully and quietly, we opened one of the windows on the side of the house. Thorny motioned Poppy and me out first and handed us some bags through the window for us to tie to our horses' saddles. It made *me* feel like a thief, and I wondered what I had done to deserve being placed in a mess like this.

When Thorny climbed out, he made a gesture with his club and then disappeared around the side of the cabin. I waited with bated breath and listened as two hard objects collided. Perhaps a second later, there was a light thump. But *who* was the thump?

A few more seconds passed. My heart pounded in my chest.

I exhaled heavily as I saw Thorny walk around the corner. "You didn't hurt him, did you?" I asked without thinking.

Thorny gave me a crooked smile. "He'll live." He tossed the club to the ground and gave a jerk of his head. "How about we get out of here before the others return?"

"Good idea," I agreed.

We started to load up Luna and Phoenix, and I saw Poppy giving us a weird look, like she wanted to say something but wasn't sure how.

"What is it?" I asked her.

"I think I should take one of the bandits' horses," she said. "It would make things faster and easier."

"Now we're going to become *horse-thieves*?" I blurted. I never knew that stealing would end up being such a slippery business.

"Stealing from thieves isn't stealing," Thorny said, crossing his arms. "I think it's a good idea."

"But it means we're stooping to their level!" I protested.

"If someone stole something from you, wouldn't you rather someone more deserving have it?" Poppy asked.

I thought Thorny was rubbing off on her too much, but I didn't have time to argue any longer. "Fine. But you are *not* taking another thing from them, even if they *are* bandits."

"Agreed," Thorny said. "We don't need anything else anyway."

"Because you practically robbed them blind," I muttered to myself in ill humor.

Poppy chose a handsome black horse with a white star on his head and white socks above his back hooves. "I'm naming you 'Prince' because you look regal," she told him.

It was all I could do to refrain from snorting.

We redistributed the saddlebags so that Prince could carry some of the weight. I mounted Luna, murmuring an apology for any ill treatment she had faced at the hands of the bandits, and waited for my other traveling companions to get on their horses.

Poppy went over to Thorny as he was putting a foot in Phoenix's stirrup. She put a hand on his arm, and he paused, giving her a questioning look.

"Thank you for saving us," she said, so softly it was hard for me to hear.

He smiled at her. "It's all part of a prince's job, isn't it? Saving damsels in distress."

I felt something twist in my gut, but I pushed the feeling away and loudly cleared my throat.

Thorny turned red. "But, ah, the one you should be thanking is Elle. We'd still be tied up if it wasn't for her."

Poppy turned her face toward me, and I saw some indefinable emotion flicker across it. Then she said: "Thank you for your help, Elle."

"The rat deserves more credit than I do," I said uncomfortably. "But I really think it's a good idea to leave now."

They nodded in assent, and a few minutes later, we were riding out of sight of the bandits' home.

This time, we decided not to travel on the road. I wasn't sure whether it would help us avoid more bandits or not, but it was worth a try. And since Thorny had a sword now, we wouldn't be completely helpless if a wild animal tried to attack us. Not that I wanted to put that to the test.

We rode as far away from the cabin as was practical before settling down for the night. While Thorny built a small fire, I watched, only to lift my head in puzzlement when I saw Poppy wander off. To avoid any embarrassments, we always planned where each of us would go to answer nature's call when we first chose a campsite. But she hadn't gone in her established direction, and I was curious about what she was doing, so I murmured something to the distracted Thorny before standing to follow my stepsister.

I snuck forward quietly. She hadn't gone far, and as I peered around a tree, I saw a bird settling down into her hands. It was making contented coos, and she was talking to it in a low voice.

While I thought it was somewhat odd, I knew she liked birds, so I simply gave a mental shrug and went back to the fire, which was now blazing brightly in the dark night. Maybe a little *too* brightly.

"You don't think the bandits will see the smoke and come find us?" I asked Thorny with a frown.

"I doubt it," he said. "We can't be the only travelers around. And I don't know what kind of wild beasts are in these parts—the fire will help scare them off, and I'd rather face a pack of bandits than a hungry bear."

I wasn't sure I agreed—weren't we traveling off the road to *avoid* the bandits?—but I nodded my acceptance.

"Umm," Thorny said, handing me the book we had recovered from the bandits, "here's this back. I don't think you got to finish reading it?"

"No, I didn't," I confirmed, looking down at it. I sort of feared what answers I might find within it now. Something about that incident with the rat . . .

A noise caught my attention, and I turned, only to find Phoenix practically on top of Luna.

"Thorny!" I gasped, pointing.

He turned and looked at the two horses, and then he grinned and let out a chuckle. "Come on, give 'em a little privacy."

"What are you talking about? Your stupid rare horse is attacking mine! *Do something!*"

"No," Thorny said, "he's just mounting—"

"What's going on?" asked an out-of-breath Poppy. "I heard yelling—"

"Thorny's horse is attacking Luna!" I exclaimed. "We have to pull them apart somehow! Can we get a bucket of water or something?"

"Wait," Thorny said, "you seriously don't . . . ?" He gave me a dumbfounded look and then turned to Poppy. "Oh, no, no, no. There's *no* way I'm explaining the mares and the steeds to my future wife."

Poppy held her hands up. "Don't look at me. You're the most qualified for this as her 'future husband!'"

"Hello," I cried out, panicking. "My horse!"

Poppy let loose an aggravated growl and grabbed my arm. "Your horse is fine. Come with me."

She took me out of Thorny's earshot to give me a talk that she declared—with aggravated emphasis—was long overdue. All the while, I could feel my face getting hotter and hotter. I had been too young when my mother had died for *her* to give me this talk, and Iris certainly wasn't about to step into that role for me.

When Poppy and I walked back to the campfire, I must have been as red as a tomato. Thorny looked at me, and I told him in a strangled voice, "Don't touch me, and for the love of all that is sacred, keep your sword sheathed."

Thorny turned to Poppy. "Just what kind of metaphor did you use, anyway?"

Poppy said sweetly, "A bloody one."

I couldn't help but shudder. Poppy had seemed especially intent on emphasizing the horrific aspects of everything, likely as vengeance against Thorny. But it certainly made me wonder why anyone would willingly procreate.

The meal we ate before bed that night passed by somewhat awkwardly. When I finally got in my pallet, I was relieved at the prospect of some rest, but my mind was so occupied by the images that Poppy had put there that I couldn't go to sleep.

I had already seen the violence of childbirth, even if my experience had been restricted to the birth of a lamb rather than a human baby, yet I hadn't thought much about applying the general idea to myself. Despite the blood and torturous pain I had seen with Soleil's lambing, I had been rather impressed by the miracle of birth at Silverthorn. Still, I had had a few dreams afterward of a screaming baby covered with blood, and it made me a little fearful of motherhood for myself. How bad did it all really hurt?

And now the issue of blood had arisen again. Poppy said that while a woman's monthly might bring cramps to the stomach, the first plunge of a man's sword came with great pain and often even blood. Why was it the lot of women to be constantly bleeding? I remembered when my cycle first began and how I had been terrified because I thought I was dying. A female servant had actually explained that one to me—I wasn't sure which one of us had been more embarrassed at the time.

It was with these thoughts in mind that I lay there in my pallet. And so I was awake to see Poppy rise from hers and tiptoe toward Thorny. She turned toward me, and I slammed my eyes shut without thinking, opening them cautiously a few seconds later.

She crept toward Thorny and kneeled on the ground, lifting a leg up and over him to straddle his lower torso.

I raised myself on my elbow so I could see her better. *What* was she *doing*?

She put her hands on opposite sides of the prince and lowered her face toward his neck. Gently, she began placing kisses along his exposed skin as she whispered his name. He shifted a little in his sleep, murmuring something, and then she slid her hands down his clothed chest and beneath his blanket.

Suddenly, his eyes shot open, and he flung Poppy off him. "Whoa! Whoa! The only one allowed to polish my sword is *me*!"

There was no point in feigning sleep now. Thorny's shout was loud enough to wake the dead.

Poppy was red-faced. She murmured, "I'm sorry. I thought you'd—"

"Don't you 'I'm sorry' me," growled Thorny. "There are some things that require mutual consent, and that is most definitely one of them."

"But I didn't even touch—"

"You came rat-nestin' close, and you ought to be ashamed of yourself!" He then went into a string of curses, finishing with, "You pixie-bit harlot!"

Poppy inclined her head, her face growing redder by the second, and then she returned to her pallet without another word.

Thorny looked at me, and I could practically hear him thinking: *This is why we should have never brought her.* But he said nothing out loud, just flopped down on his belly and threw his cover over his head, muttering something to himself.

I nestled back into my own sleeping pallet, my heart pounding, though I had done nothing wrong. I felt terrible for Thorny—and angry at Poppy—but that small scene was enough to set my mind whirling. Poppy had made the act of creating life sound so horrific and violent . . . yet that wasn't what this scene had appeared like, even if it was one-sided. Why couldn't child-making be full of caresses and kisses? Was it really to be so feared?

When I finally went to sleep that night, I had a dream where I was on a bed that was covered with rose petals, and Thorny was sitting on top of me, placing hundreds of soft kisses along my neck as I whispered his name.

CHAPTER 10:
TORRENTS

hen we woke up in the morning, the tension in the air was so thick it was almost suffocating. Thorny was taking every chance he could to glare at Poppy, and she was avoiding both his gaze and mine with all she had.

We ate a quick breakfast and began traveling again. We were fortunate that New Fountain was actually fairly close to the Airland border. If we traveled to the nearby city of Palewater, we *could* use the bridge there to go over the river. However, since the city was so close to Airland, as Thorny noted, they were likely to ask a lot of questions about travelers' intentions. In addition, Palewater was also close to the capital, and though the capital was beyond the river, it still made things a little bit trickier.

When we settled down for the night and took one last look at Thorny's maps, we determined that we would cross the river the next day without using the Palewater bridge. That was the main extent of our verbal communication that night—I had apologized in private about Poppy's actions, but Thorny's figurative fur was still ruffled, and I didn't push for him and Poppy to reconcile. I figured they needed some time.

When we reached the river in the morning, we discovered a problem. This was no tame stream, but a raging danger of rapids and sharp stones. How were we supposed to cross it?

"Maybe there's a tree near the river that we can cut down somehow," Thorny said. A roll of thunder punctuated his words. It looked like it was going to rain soon.

"We could go to the bridge," Poppy pointed out.

"The bridge will have guards," Thorny said, "and I don't want my father to know what I'm doing. There's a chance I could be recognized."

Yes, his father wouldn't want him to know he was traipsing around the kingdom with a couple of commoners, would he? I shook the thought away and said, "Even if we're fortunate enough to find a dead tree to push over, that doesn't mean we can get the horses across."

"Fortunately, those are all problems you don't have to worry about right now," said a new voice.

The three of us swiveled around in surprise.

Standing before us was a strange-looking man. He was wearing odd clothes made up of animal skins and a hat topped with feathers from exotic birds. Though his light brown hair was barely visible, I could tell it was flecked with gray, which made it appear like the mottled fur of some wild cat. I recognized him instantly.

His name was Birch Treeson. When my stepmother had been able to afford taking time out of her day to chase wild game in the woods, he was her huntsman. I was certain he had once been handsome, but something that had happened in his past had given him a slightly feral look.

"Good day, Miss Beauregard and Miss Labelle," he said, bowing slightly to us. Then he turned to Thorny and gave a much more exaggerated bow. "Your Highness."

I looked at Thorny in surprise. How did Treeson know who he was?

Thorny's voice was like iron. "What are you doing here, Treeson? I'm surprised your head hasn't made it to an executioner's block yet."

Treeson gave him a hurt look. "Now, now, young cub, there's no need for that. In spite of everything that has happened, your sire still has a dear spot in his heart for his good old hunting buddy."

"What are you talking about?" I blurted.

"Oh," said the huntsman dismissively, "it was a silly little incident. I was merely trying to help young Thorny kill his first bear. That was all."

"That was *not* all," Thorny growled. "I was eight and didn't know how to swim. There was a bear trying to catch fish in the stream. My father's 'trusted huntsman' told me the currents weren't very strong." His eyes glinted in anger. "He was wrong."

Treeson shrugged. "I never understood what the

big commotion was about. I fished the young prince out."

"You left me to drown," snarled Thorny. "If that log hadn't been there, I would have died."

Treeson waved his hand. "Oh, I would've come after you eventually."

"It doesn't matter," said Thorny in a tight voice. "Tell me, why are you here?"

"Questions are such pesky things. I much prefer dead animals to live humans. At least dead animals never have anything to say."

"Well, you're just about as interesting and repulsive as a dead rat, so that's fitting," snapped Thorny.

"Tell you what," said Birch Treeson thoughtfully, as if an idea had just occurred to him, "how about we fight in the river? If you win, I'll leave you alone forever."

"I wouldn't give you the pleasure of me stooping to your level to fight!"

"I worried you might say that," said Treeson, pulling out a pistol. They weren't great at long-range, but the three of us were all within its firing distance, and he was pointing it at me. "If you don't fight me, I'll shoot this pretty little filly in the head. And then I'll carve out her heart."

"You sick—"

"Uh, uh, uh," said the huntsman. "No name-calling. Now, after you." He gestured to the river with the gun.

"Thorny, this isn't a good idea," I said, worried that the prince's masculine pride was going to get him killed. Surely Birch Treeson wouldn't shoot me in cold blood.

But Thorny ignored me and looked at Treeson.

"No, after *you*."

The huntsman glanced at the river. It wasn't deep in this spot, but the current was probably strong enough to knock him over the moment he stepped in the water. He must have realized that, as he reconsidered his challenge. "I've changed my mind," he said. "Let's not fight here. There's a fallen tree hanging across the river a little ways down from this spot that I use to cross at my leisure. How about we make this more interesting and fight on top of it?"

Thorny's gaze was hard. "Fine. But I have to warn you that I'm a lot stronger than that kid you used to wrestle with."

Treeson laughed. "I've slow-danced with bears, boy. A young sprout such as you is nothing for me to fear."

Thorny's eyes glinted. "Perhaps you have. But have you ever fought a wolf?"

"Ha!" laughed the huntsman. "You're no wolf, boy."

"I wouldn't be so sure," Thorny murmured.

As Birch Treeson led us to the fallen tree he had spoken of, I tried to convince Thorny to reason with the huntsman. But the threat to me had made the prince's blood boil, and my pleas fell on deaf ears. I attempted to get Poppy to help me, but she seemed bothered by something—maybe fear of Treeson—and didn't want to talk. There was a part of me that wanted to rush at Treeson and attempt to wrestle the gun away, but the more time ticked by, the more certain I was that he would actually use the weapon on me if I tried anything.

When we arrived at our destination, Treeson deftly

hopped on the fallen tree and gave Thorny an expectant look.

The prince handed Phoenix's reins to me, a grim look on his face. It seemed he was just as aware as I was that our situation was a dire one.

I clenched Thorny's hand on impulse and gazed sternly into his eyes. "You have to promise you'll come back to me, Thorny."

He gave me a crooked smile and brought up his other hand to cover mine. I curled my fingers between his palms and stared downward, unsure of what else to say.

"I promise we'll be together again, Elle," he said, and I looked up at him. He lifted a hand to brush the hair out of my face, and his fingers lingered briefly on my cheek before withdrawing. I reached up to touch the place on my skin that he had caressed, and I watched as he moved to climb on top of the tree trunk.

"A count of five, and then we begin?" suggested the huntsman once his opponent was in place.

Thorny nodded, his face tight and arms held ready.

"One," said Treeson.

I saw Poppy turn away out of the corner of my eye.

"Two," the huntsman said, gazing at the water foaming beneath him. Or so I thought. I realized too late that he wasn't looking at the water. Rather, he was looking at Thorny's feet. And as he said "three," he swept out a leg and knocked Thorny off the trunk. I barely managed to catch the prince's look of surprise before he was carried away downstream.

"Thorny!" I screamed, rushing forward. But even though Treeson jumped forward to grab me and keep me from jumping in, I realized quickly there was nothing I could do—the river was moving too fast. To go in after Thorny would be suicide.

I looked at Treeson in fury. "You cheater!"

He gave a nauseating smile as he tightened his grip on me. "I never claimed I would play by the rules. Besides, your prince is an excellent swimmer."

"No, he isn't!" I said, trying to tear myself away from him.

"Oops," said Treeson with a wide-eyed look as he dug his fingers into my arm. "I guess I forgot about that little incident where he nearly drowned. Oh, well. It's a pity."

"You're heartless," I spat.

The huntsman raised an eyebrow. "Am I? Well, let me tell you that my lot in life hasn't been a good one since your pretty stepmother lost all her money. I've been stuck doing odd jobs—it seems my stigma of nearly killing a prince has stuck with most people even if it didn't with dear Iris Beauregard. At least now I can be banned for something I actually did."

I glared up at him. "If he's dead, I'll—"

"You'll what?" countered Treeson. "Threats from little girls don't frighten me. Especially not when it's a little girl I'm supposed to kill."

"What?" I blurted. Who would want *me* dead? The king? But why would Treeson have pushed *Thorny* into the river?

"Yes, I'm supposed to kill you. You're my real job. The prince was just a nice bonus."

"You can't kill her!" exclaimed Poppy.

"Oh, but I can. I'm supposed to bring back her heart or some such. Perfectly beastly, isn't it?" He sighed. "Unfortunately, I believe she's too pretty to kill. For some reason, I've always had a soft spot for pretty women."

I wasn't sure whether to be relieved or annoyed. He let go of my arm, and I asked, "Is that really why you're letting me go?"

He turned serious for a brief instant. "Perhaps I saw you once crying and talking to your horse. Perhaps it reminded me of someone, and I thought I would one day do you a good turn if I could." He turned and looked at Luna. He never rode horses, which I had always thought odd, but his great endurance and sure feet meant he didn't need to. Still, I knew he had a strange affinity with animals, even if he was always killing them.

"But you must go on to Airland and never return," he said, "or I will start the hunt again." He tipped his hat and left without another word.

I looked up at the dark clouds gathering in the sky. This wasn't good weather for a manhunt, but I was not about to abandon Thorny to the river if I could help it. There was a chance that those doggy-paddling lessons I had given him when he was a wolf would help him stay alive.

"Come on," I said to Poppy, taking Phoenix's reins. I knew Luna would follow me. "Get your horse. We're going to look for Thorny." A couple of raindrops fell on my head, and I tilted my head back to let a few drip onto my face. I would much rather concentrate on the thought of rain than attempt to determine who might want me dead—or consider the thought that Thorny might have drowned in the river. I told myself I was going to find him, and he was going to be alive. There was no other option.

"All right," Poppy said.

We went down the riverbank, looking for any sign of Thorny or his passing—a shoe, a wet mop of hair, *anything*. Meanwhile, the rain picked up its pace and was soon falling in sheets so thick that it was hard to see two feet in front of me.

"We're never going to find Thorny in this rain," Poppy shouted through the downpour.

"Don't say that!" I shouted back, drenched and shivering. "We're going to find him!" Yes, the visibility was poor, but we would find Thorny. We *would*.

As I blinked the water out of my eyes, I noticed a gleaming light. I took in a quick breath. *Thorny?*

The lantern came closer, and I saw it was carried by an old dwarf. It was hard to make out much in the rain, but I could see that his other hand clutched an iron staff with a spike on the end.

The staff seemed somewhat threatening, but I was desperate. If there was a chance he had any information about Thorny, I had to know.

"Excuse me, sir," I shouted. "Have you seen a young man who got washed down the river?"

He continued moving toward us and said in a kind voice, "Yes, young lady. I have seen your young man. He is safe. Come with me—I've got shelter from the storm."

"You've . . . you've seen Thorny?" I asked hopefully.

"Yes," he said, blinking up at me through the rain.

"I don't like this, Elle," Poppy murmured by my ear.

"We've got to go see, Poppy," I told her. Then,

speaking to the dwarf loudly, I said, "Lead the way."

He smiled and nodded. After adjusting the large hat on his head, he limped forward and led us into the forest. It was nice to have a little cover from the rain, but I was so worried about Thorny it was hard to appreciate it. And then finally, I saw it—the mottled and disarrayed ruins of a castle. A small castle, to be sure, but the design intent of the stones was clear, and the structure seemed intact enough to provide shelter.

"That looks really creepy, Elle," Poppy hissed behind me. "I've got a bad feeling about this."

CHAPTER 11:
SEVEN HUNGRY DWARVES

As we went into the first part of the castle, I was able to get a closer look at the dwarf. He had a bushy white beard that came midway down his chest, and though it was quite wet, I could tell he must have kept it well-groomed. His clothes were even more interesting, however—he wore a bright red hat, iron-shod boots, and an antique-looking tunic.

"You're sure you've seen Thorny?" I asked, wanting to make certain once more.

"Yes," he told me with a smile. "Now, you can leave your horses in the foyer. They'll be protected from the rain there."

"Are you certain?" I asked. "It's not too much of an imposition?" I hated leaving the horses *inside* the castle, but I also didn't want to leave them out in the rain.

He nodded and said warmly, "It's not a problem. You two look soaked to the bone. You must come in and dry yourselves by the fire. My name is Red. I know the boys will be glad to see you."

After introducing ourselves, Poppy and I took a moment to tend to the horses before following Red deeper into the castle.

He led us to a large open room where six other dwarves were gathered around a large fire. They were talking and laughing, and though their beards and tunics were different colors, they all wore iron-shod boots and red caps. While it was generally considered impolite to wear hats inside, the outside world had intruded enough upon the castle's ruins that it didn't seem too strange. There were plants growing here and there in dirt-filled holes beside broken stones, and large patches of moss covered several walls. Add to that the general damp atmosphere and the flickering of the fire, and it felt almost like we were in a cave.

"Lost travelers?" one of the dwarves called out upon seeing us.

"Actually, sir, we're *looking* for someone, not *lost*," I corrected. "Thank you for providing shelter from the storm, but I thought . . . I thought my friend might be here?"

"No, we thank you for livening up the party," returned Red. "And don't worry—we'll discuss your young man soon enough. Now, my companions are Genta, Rou, Roon, Burgun, Verm, and Crim." He pointed them out as he said their names, and I watched politely as he did.

I glanced at Poppy, who seemed determined not to speak, and then, for lack of anything better to say, I told them, "You have nice hats."

"Thanks," a small dwarf piped up. "We're pretty attached to them ourselves."

"And just by being here, you brighten up our lives," another tittered.

"We feel rosy already," said one who didn't look happy in the slightest.

"Please forgive my friends," said Red, frowning. "We don't get nearly as many visitors as we'd like here."

"You actually *live* here?" I exclaimed.

"Yes," said the dwarf with a fond glance at his surroundings. "It's a bit drafty and damp, perhaps, but it gives us plenty of room to do what we want."

"We were about to prepare a meal," said the dour dwarf who had made the rosy comment. "You're welcome to partake in it." Never mind that he didn't look particularly welcoming.

"Oh, we wouldn't want to impose any more than we already have," I told him, holding my hands up. "And I really would just like to see my—"

"We insist," he interrupted, looking over at the other dwarf. "You wouldn't want to offend old Crim, now would you?" For a moment, his eyes seemed to gleam in the light given off by the fire.

"No," I said, resisting the urge to shiver as Crim stared at me. "I guess I wouldn't."

So I watched (with Poppy practically clinging to me) as the red-capped dwarves cooked and brought in tables that they piled countless items of food on. They had not even finished cooking before they started urging Poppy and me to eat. They brought out a few chairs and pushed us into them, Red saying all the while, "Our guests mustn't go hungry. We must feed them plenty of food to help sustain their poor little bodies."

"Yes, they could use a little more flesh on them," Crim agreed.

Poppy and I exchanged an uneasy look. "You know," I said, "I think you should just take us to my friend now." I kept trying to remind them of him, but they seemed determined to feed Poppy and me before they did anything of the sort.

"Nonsense," said one of the dwarves. "You must forgive old Crim. Poor fellow's always surly. You must indulge yourselves before you go out to face that dreadful weather."

"You mean he's not here?" I asked, disappointed and even a little uneasy.

"Sorry," said a dwarf, spreading his hands out in an apologetic gesture. "Your friend *was* here, but now he's gone."

"Well," said Red, "that *is* a shame. But I'm sure we can reunite you with him after you eat."

That was the last thing I wanted, but if Thorny really had escaped the river, then rushing out into the storm wouldn't help him. I didn't like it, but I felt like my hands were tied.

"Well," I said, looking back toward the exit, "I guess we can have just a few bites. But then we need to go."

"Yes, yes," Red said happily.

So Poppy and I began to eat, though I had lost most of my appetite and suspected she had, too.

Something made me uncomfortable about how all the dwarves were eyeing us and trying to coax us to eat more and more despite what I had said. But when I finally couldn't stand one more bite, I said, "I'm full now, really. Thank you so much for your hospitality, but we have to leave to find our friend."

"Oh, no," said Red, looking alarmed, "you mustn't go now. Please, you must rest and then eat some more. Both of you look so puny—all this traveling must be making you famished."

"No," I said. Poppy's fingers were digging into my arm like talons, and I knew she was terrified. "We must insist on going. I'm sorry."

"We're sorry, too," Red said sadly, and I watched, paralyzed with fear, as Crim moved toward me with his pike staff held high. What I didn't see was the dwarf that snuck up behind me and knocked me out.

When I came to, I had a raging headache, and Poppy was screaming her lungs out. After a few painful yet groggy seconds, I realized I was tied to a long pole and being carried over to the fire to be roasted. They meant to eat me!

I began to panic. I threw my body this way and that. I struggled to slip my hands out of their bonds. And then something strange happened. Some of the flames jumped out of the fire and onto my body.

"No, no!" I whimpered, struggling even more. I didn't want to burn to death.

But the flames that had jumped on me weren't

hurting me. Instead, they were eating away at the ropes that bound me. And then, suddenly, I fell off the pole and onto the ground.

"Fairies!" cried Crim. "We've caught fairies!"

I lifted my head off the floor, blinking in confusion. The dwarves had dropped the pole and were backing away from me as though I could smite them with a glance. Wincing from the force of my fall, I got to my feet and hobbled over to Poppy, who was tied to a chair. But before I could free her, the flames leaped from my body and began burning away her bonds. The pitch of Poppy's shrieks rose even higher.

Seconds later, after my stepsister was freed, the fire returned to me. The dwarves were clenching their pike staffs and obviously trying to decide whether to rush me. For some reason, I thought of a book I had once read aloud to Thorny at Silverthorn, and it inspired me.

"I am not a fairy," I said, raising my arms up in what I hoped was an intimidating pose, "but a powerful witch."

The dwarves looked wary, but not quite frightened like I had hoped, so I made a flinging motion to try to scare them. The gesture actually sent all the fire flying, and it flared up in a circle around the seven dwarves, who cried out in fear.

"Don't follow us," I shouted, "or I shall be very displeased!" And then I yanked a bug-eyed Poppy by the arm, grabbed our belongings, and fled the room.

Poppy didn't need any encouragement to saddle her horse, and soon we were galloping away from that ruined castle like we were both on fire.

"I didn't know you were a fairy," Poppy gasped

once we were out of sight of the castle. It was still raining, though not as hard as it had been.

"I'm not a fairy," I said, but I wasn't so sure. What exactly *had* happened back there?

She didn't argue with me, likely too surprised at our escape to make much more effort to communicate.

We had not ridden very far before I called to Poppy to slow Prince to a trot. The rain was picking back up again, and we needed to be careful not to exhaust our horses. I also didn't want Luna to lose sight of Phoenix since I was counting on her to follow us.

A flash of lightning highlighted a dark figure mere feet away, and Phoenix reared up in the air. For a moment, I feared I was going to be tossed off. I clung to his neck in desperation. Finally, his hooves hit the ground again.

"Elle?" the form asked in surprise.

I squinted. "Thorny?" And then I knew for certain it was him, and I jumped off and threw myself at him. We fell to the ground.

"Thorny!" I sobbed into his shoulder, holding onto him as if I wouldn't ever let go.

Though he had been surprised when I launched myself at him, he tightened his arms around me. "Elle," he breathed. "I thought you were dead. I've been so worried."

"And I feared the same about you! When I saw that river take you—"

"Hey, hey, I'm all right now. There's no need to worry anymore."

"Thorny—"

"What's that?" squealed Poppy suddenly.

I sat up in alarm and looked where she was

pointing. Standing a short distance away was a distinctly wolflike form, and I wondered how I had missed it.

Thorny—still lying on the ground—twisted his head and body so he could see where my attention was.

"Is that your mother?" I asked, though I didn't think it was. The wolf looked silver, not red, and I didn't think Queen Rose would have just stood there quietly in the rain, though I admittedly wasn't well acquainted with her.

"No," said Thorny, returning his gaze to me, "that's Slate."

"Slate?"

"Much though I enjoy this position, can we get out of the rain and mud first and then talk?" he asked.

"All right," I said, slowly moving off him, embarrassed that I had knocked him to the muddy ground.

Poppy didn't say anything else, but I saw the tension in her face as she watched the wolf.

Thorny and I mounted our horses, which shifted nervously, eyeing Slate. Fortunately, the wolf showed no interest in them.

"Slate," said Thorny, "can you lead us to a cave or something where we can get out of the rain?"

The silver wolf looked at Thorny for a few seconds, his eyes gleaming, and then he turned and began briskly walking away.

Thorny followed him on Phoenix without hesitation, and Poppy and I brought our horses after him, though I could tell that we both had some reservations about trusting a wild animal. All things considered, I should have been more willing, yet so much had happened in such a short time that I was leery of trusting anything.

The wolf took us to a small cave embedded in a large bank. It was tall enough for our horses, but not very deep. Still, it was perfect for what we needed.

Thorny and I dismounted, but Poppy hesitated. "I don't trust that thing," she said, curling her fingers more tightly around her horse's reins.

"It's all right," I said. "He won't hurt you." At least, I didn't *think* he would. Surely Thorny of all people would be able to gauge whether a wolf was a threat or not.

Poppy finally got down, but she placed herself as far from Slate as was feasible. The wolf, meanwhile, simply lay down, put his head on his paws, and closed his eyes. His ears, however, seemed alert, twitching periodically. I wondered if that was how Thorny had slept as a wolf, and I frowned as I realized that I had never been curious enough to try to find out at Silverthorn.

While Thorny built a fire, I watched warily. I had no desire to be anywhere *near* flames again after what had happened with the dwarves, but we *did* need to get dry.

"Thank you, Your Highness," murmured Poppy, which I guessed was her attempt to reconcile with the prince after their earlier spat about proper boundaries.

"Yeah," Thorny replied, which must have been his way of saying he accepted her apology with some reluctance.

I rolled my eyes. "So, can you tell us about your new furry friend?"

Thorny looked over at Slate. The wolf's ears had moved when I spoke, but he didn't open his eyes. Softly, the prince said, "He saved my life."

"How could a beast save your life?" Poppy asked. She was genuinely interested, but the flash of annoyance in Thorny's eyes told me she should have chosen her words more carefully.

Surprisingly, the prince managed to hold on to his temper. "Doggy-paddling isn't always easy to do when a river throws you around like a ragdoll among a million rocks. I was going to drown—I *know* I was—when Slate jumped into the river and saved me. I didn't realize what he was doing at first—I thought maybe he figured me to be easy prey—but I threw my arms around him anyway, and he swam us both to the shore."

We all looked at the silver wolf then. He was large but thin, and I resolved to give him a good meal of rabbit or deer if I could somehow manage it.

"I remembered you call male animals after stones," Thorny said, "so I named him 'Slate.' It felt like I had to call him something, you know? Especially when he started following me around."

"Where did you go?" I asked.

"I went to Palewater when I couldn't find you. I thought maybe you'd go there if Treeson hadn't killed you. Slate refused to come inside the city—I thought he meant to leave me for good, so I said farewell and thanked him."

"What did you do in the city?" Poppy asked.

"I went to an inn and tried to figure out whether anyone had seen you. That was when I heard about the redcaps."

"Redcaps?" Poppy echoed.

"Yeah. People said they're lightning-fast dwarves that control the weather. They lure travelers into their ruined castles, where they fatten and eat them. I think maybe those castles act like faelanxes for evil spirits."

"Faelanxes?" I repeated. My stepmother had used that term, but I didn't know what it meant.

"One of the marked passages in that *On Fairies* book talks about faelanxes. Faelanxes are places that spirits are attracted to. I think that spirits are what redcaps use to control the weather. They sound rather nasty. They are supposed to wear red hats which they dye in their victims' blood, and it's said that their lives end whenever the blood dries out. When I heard rumors that redcaps are living in the ruins of a castle nearby, I left the city to save you, and Slate rejoined me. He actually led me to you."

My stomach twisted as I thought of how those redcaps had nearly consumed Poppy and me. "Well," I said, "we almost didn't get out of that castle alive."

Thorny's eyes widened. "So there *were* redcaps?"

"Yeah," said Poppy, "but Elle took care of them."

Thorny frowned. "What do you mean?"

I gave Poppy a warning look. "It was nothing."

"She saved us by throwing fire at them," Poppy said, ignoring me. "We would've been burned alive otherwise."

"Throwing fire?" said Thorny, an eyebrow raised.

"I don't know how it happened," I said. I held my chin high, trying to will him not to press the issue. But even as I did so, I fully expected him to ask more questions. To my surprise, however, he simply frowned thoughtfully and kept quiet.

"The rain's lifting up," Poppy observed.

Thorny and I looked out of the cave. The rain had all but stopped.

"How about we all go to Palewater?" Thorny suggested. "The innkeeper at *The Booted Cat* seems friendly enough, and the food smells good. I'd say we deserve a break from our travels in the woods to have a real meal and rest our feet." But he was looking at me questioningly. Even though he had a pouch of golden Oaks entirely at his disposal, I had become the one in charge of our funds.

I chuckled to myself at the thought. "Sure, that sounds good to me. But will Slate be sad that we're going into the city without him?"

"I'm pretty sure he can control his heartbreak," Thorny said dryly. "Wolves can't get sad anyway."

I didn't disagree with him, but I knew that they could, and so did he.

As I climbed up on my horse, I saw Thorny giving Slate a questioning look, as if for approval, and I smiled to myself.

CHAPTER 12:
MAGICALLY MALICIOUS

he innkeeper at *The Booted Cat* was indeed a kind woman. Before we went inside the inn, Thorny explained that everyone called her "Madam Feline," no doubt because of the countless cats patrolling the establishment. But while I would have thought the cats would deter people from coming to her inn, all of Madam Feline's patrons seemed at home. As we entered, I saw a man playing cards in the back with one hand on his cards and another dangling to pet a cat's head. A few more glances around the room revealed that many a lap had a small furry body in it.

Upon seeing us, a woman who could only be Madam Feline cried out: "Oh, the poor dears! You are soaked to the bone!" And then, alternately cooing and clucking over the state of our wet clothes, she ushered the three of us into chairs at a long table and pushed mugs of warm cider into our hands.

A cat almost immediately jumped into my lap, and as I stroked it, Madam Feline smiled and said, "Let me get you some hot soup."

When she brought the soup over, I told her, "Thank you so much."

She beamed. "It's my pleasure, dear. Your young man has been so worried about you. I'm glad he was able to bring you here safely."

I flushed and picked up a spoon. Poppy and Thorny, who were on the opposite side of the table from me, had already begun eating. While I tried to take bites slowly so I could savor the flavor, the vegetables in the soup were so soft and tasty that it was hard to resist gulping the whole bowl down just as my companions were doing. Carrots, celery, potatoes, beef, noodles—these were a few of the items I could most easily pick out, and each bite was delightful. Traveling rations were definitely *not* meant for taste the way this was. And it had been hard to enjoy the meal provided by those bloodthirsty dwarves, no matter *how* good the food had looked.

After Poppy had a few helpings, she was finished, though Thorny looked like he could go for a while yet. He was shoveling food in his mouth with one hand while the other rested on the table.

Poppy had only been done eating for a few minutes when she reached up to rest a hand on the prince's immobile fingers.

He smacked her hand off his and snarled, "Stop it!"

"Stop what?" she asked innocently.

He just growled beneath his breath.

I turned my attention back to my food and finished the bowl, trying not to snicker.

A few minutes later, Thorny put his spoon down, and a man with a scarred lip and bushy black hair ambled over.

"I see your young ladies weren't eaten by the redcaps after all," the stranger said.

"It was a close one," I said. "They seemed like such nice dwarves."

The man nodded, unsurprised that I had come across the vicious dwarves. "That they do. It's how they lure their meals in, you know. Makes them good predators." He leaned on top of an empty chair at our table. "So where are you three off to now?"

"Oh, leave the poor young folks alone, Linden," someone called.

But the man didn't move, and Thorny answered, "We're trying to find the Arm of Avalon."

I tried to give Thorny a warning look—it probably wasn't the best idea to announce our travel plans—but he was gazing at Linden instead of me, so he failed to see my expression.

Linden smiled, showing a mouth with a few teeth missing. "You're hoping to make one of your young ladies queen, aren't you? We know all about those stories, being near the border of Airland and all."

"Oh, leave off those legends," said the same man who had called out for Linden not to bother us.

But again, Linden ignored him. "Do you have a map?"

Thorny nodded and pulled out a map of Airland from one of his pockets. He unfolded it and placed it on the table, setting some cutlery on the corners to keep it flat.

Linden looked at the map and then began sliding a dirty forefinger along it. "You pass into Airland, and then you go here, where you'll find a circle of mountains surrounding a valley. You have to cross over one of the mountains, and then at the base, you'll find that the land is craggy and filled with chimeras. Remember, their fiery breath can burn off flesh, so don't let your guard down. Once you make it past them, you'll come to a forest which surrounds the lake. And in that forest are the legendary garms—bloodstained watchdogs that'll tear off your face as soon as they see you."

Madam Feline was standing nearby and clucked in disapproval. "You mustn't go face all those nasty creatures," she said. "I hear the garms have an especially big appetite for cats. Wretched beasts!"

"But if you make it through all that," continued Linden as if there hadn't been an interruption, "you'll come upon the beautiful lake. And resting in those waters is the mysterious Lady of the Lake."

"Such a tragic figure," said Madam Feline, dabbing her eyes with a handkerchief that she pulled out of the top of her dress. "She was a beautiful fairy whose true love drowned in the lake before they were married. So she walked into the lake and was never heard from again."

"That's what some say," acknowledged Linden. "But others claim she's simply a spirit or a witch—or even a monster. Still others claim it is Queen Avalon herself, guarding the sword that will bequeath her kingdom to its next ruler."

I looked down at the map uneasily. Linden's sausage of a finger completely covered Lake Avalon, which seemed awfully small compared to the mountains and forest surrounding it. Maybe this was my chance to convince Thorny to drop me off in Airland and quit this quest. The guilt I felt about leaving him was growing larger the closer we got to Airland, and I wasn't sure I would really be able to do what I had originally planned.

A short man with a bad leg hobbled over. He had been listening intently the whole time. "Tell them what happens after getting the sword."

Linden smiled. I had the feeling he was a resident storyteller of sorts for the inn, though obviously some of the inn's regulars did not tolerate him as well as others. "Once you reach the lake, you must stay away from the water's edge—if you go into it, the great lady may pull you under. If that happens, you'll never be seen again."

"But what are you *supposed* to do at the lake?" Thorny asked.

"One of your female friends needs to ask for the Arm of Avalon. Whenever a woman receives the sword, she has to take it to the Patient Steward, who'll ensure she is crowned queen. After the coronation, there's a ceremony. Right by the border between Magnolia and Airland, but on Airland's side, there's a pedestal, and that's where the ceremony takes place."

"A pedestal?" I repeated, my interest piqued. Thorny hadn't mentioned that.

"Yes. The queen takes the Arm of Avalon and plunges it into the pedestal. On the pedestal is an inscription:

"Only he whose heart is pure,
Whose spirit is selfless,
And whose body is willing and sure
May take in marriage the queen's hand
By removing the Arm of Avalon
And becoming king of all the land."

Poppy tilted her head. "So it chooses who the queen may marry?"

"Aye," said Linden. "It's a burden any Queen of Airland must be willing to carry. Many men, young and old, will try to remove the sword from the stone, and the queen does not know who shall succeed . . . or whether any shall."

"Sounds like she gets the raw end of the deal," I said dryly.

Linden shrugged. "Well, the sword *is* good at choosing a worthy young man. But sometimes the wait for such a man can cause the queen to grow too accustomed to not sharing her power. It's not a guaranteed 'happily ever after,' unfortunately."

"Well, thank you for the story," I said. "You've given us a lot to think about."

After a few more words, our storyteller and audience started to go on about their own business. I had barely even believed the Arm of Avalon had ever existed, but now it was starting to feel more real. Still, if all these stories really were true, then putting a hand on such a sword was going to be anything but easy. It shouldn't have mattered to me—I didn't intend to pursue it into the depths of garm-infested forests—but I still felt uneasy.

"Thorny," I said, "how about we just cross the river by bridge? If we smudge some dirt on your face, no one will ever recognize you."

"That fallen tree—" he began.

"—will never hold our horses' weight. And you fell off it once. Wouldn't it be better not to tempt fate?"

"But what about Slate?" he asked.

"I think it would be better to leave him behind," Poppy said. "Wolves are dangerous."

But as I looked at Thorny, I could see he was torn. And even if I tended to be attached to domestic animals rather than wild ones, how could I forget the way I had once befriended a wolf myself?

"Let's go see if he's still waiting," I suggested. "Then we can go from there."

Thorny agreed, and while I could tell Poppy wasn't pleased, she didn't protest. We gave ourselves a little more time to rest, and then we left *The Booted Cat* with Madam Feline's teary farewell in our ears.

We found Slate waiting near where we had left him, and Thorny threw down a few beefy ribs he had procured from the inn. Slate, rather than tearing into them as I would have expected, sat and began eating them with dignity.

I smiled and tugged on Luna's reins, guiding her over so I could face Thorny. He was gazing fondly down at the wolf, only to flush when he caught me looking at him.

"I have an idea," I said, not intending to comment

on his feelings for the animal. "Why don't you and Slate go across the fallen tree? Poppy and I can take the horses across the bridge."

Thorny opened his mouth to respond, only to suddenly wrinkle his nose in disgust. "What's that smell?"

On impulse, I looked upward. Then I gasped.

Up in the air was a flock of the most disturbing sort of flying creature I had ever seen. Their heads looked like human heads, but they had feathers in place of hair and beaks in place of noses. And they smelled. Really, really bad.

As the filthy creatures came closer, screaming at us, I had to put a hand up to my nose. They smelled so bad that even flies couldn't have shown an interest in them.

"Harpies," groaned Thorny, taking out his sword and putting his free hand on his saddle. "The bandits must have planted a florafruit tree nearby."

"A what?" I asked, eyeing the birds warily.

"It's a citrus fruit they're obsessed with—it's got a strong scent, and they like to cover themselves with the juices. Even *they* can't stand how bad they smell."

He might have said more, but the harpies began swooping down on us, and the chaos began.

The first one went for Poppy, who jerked Prince out of the way, shrieking, "Don't kill me! Don't touch me! Eww, eww, eww!"

Meanwhile, Thorny was trying to hack through the flurry of feathers, and I had unfastened a saddlebag and was alternating between swinging it and using it as a barrier. As for the horses, they were all going nuts, and it was hard to stay in our saddles.

"Why are they attacking us?" I shouted. "Do they eat humans?"

"They prefer their prey already d—" Thorny began to shout back, only to cut off abruptly.

I heard a thud and turned to look through an opening in the mass of infuriated harpies. Thorny had fallen to the ground, and Slate was leaping toward him.

"Thorny!" I shouted in a panic.

But rather than attack, the wolf simply covered the prince's body with his own, as if to protect him.

I was off Luna in an instant and rushed to the prince's side. Slate stared at me, and I could see the wild look in his eyes, but then he shifted a little to allow me access to Thorny.

I glanced to the side as Luna rushed off, likely to join Phoenix, who had run away once his rider had fallen to the ground. Then I looked back down at Thorny. I wasn't sure if he had been badly hurt or not, but there wasn't time to figure it out.

I grabbed the sword that had fallen beside him and began swinging it at the harpies. One screeched as the blade connected with its torso.

"Poppy!" I yelled. She was frantically guiding Prince around in an attempt to evade the stinking birds. "Did you grab some weird fruit from the bandits' house?"

"No!" she called back. "All I—eep! All I grabbed was s-some citrus perfume! Ewww, don't touch me!"

Of course, I thought. "Poppy, do you still have the bottle with you?"

"Y-yeah," she squeaked.

"Throw it on the ground *hard* and break it," I instructed her. Pointing, I added, "Then ride that way as fast as you can. I'll follow you."

I ran toward her, knowing Slate would protect Thorny, and I slashed at screeching harpies to buy my stepsister time to dig through her saddlebags. And then she found the bottle of perfume and threw it.

When the glass shattered on the ground, the effect was almost instantaneous. As one, the harpies all descended on the shards, forming a single filthy shrieking mass.

I ran to Thorny, only to realize a second wolf had joined Slate in protecting him. That in itself wasn't especially surprising. This one, however, was red.

CHAPTER 13:
EMPOWERED

re you ready, Rapunzel?" Queen Rose asked, keeping a wary eye on the harpies. "We're going to need to move fast. I would transform into a roc, but I doubt you could lift my son onto my back. And my claws would be too sharp to carry him."

"I'm ready," I confirmed.

With a flash, she transformed into her human form. We each took an end of the prince—I got his legs—and rushed toward the place where Poppy had disappeared.

As we moved further away, the harpies' cries became more muted, and I was brought to a gradual awareness of the numerous wounds covering my head and arms from the pecks and claws of the vicious birds. At another time, I might have complained or allowed myself the luxury to examine my wounds more closely, but Thorny's life was on the line, and I would have taken a hundred more pecks if it would save him.

The queen finally told me to stop walking, and she and I lowered Thorny to the ground. I called out Poppy's name, hoping she would hear and come to us. Then I returned my attention to the ground.

Queen Rose was kneeling beside Thorny, with Slate hovering nearby protectively, and as I gazed down at the prince, I couldn't help but notice that he didn't seem to be breathing.

"Thorny," I whispered, watching anxiously, my eyes filling up with tears which I shakily wiped away. What had happened? Was this how it was all going to end?

The queen skimmed a hand across Thorny's forehead and brushed the air out of his eyes. There was a mother's love in the caress, and while I might not have always agreed with her treatment of her son, it was obvious she did care for him.

When she finally stood, she gave me a reassuring smile and said, "He's not dead."

I exhaled a breath I hadn't realized I was holding. "Did one of the harpies get him? What's wrong with him, Your Majesty?"

"Please, just call me 'Rose,'" she said.

I opened my mouth to protest, only to close it at the sound of hoofbeats. I turned and found Poppy riding toward us.

"You're safe," my stepsister said in relief. "Is . . . is Thorny all right?"

As Poppy drew nearer, Queen Rose gestured at her

son. "See how the wolf is trying to protect him? That's how you can be sure he is still alive; if he weren't, the wolf would leave him."

"How do you know that?" Poppy asked.

"The wolf is his soul-brother," I answered suddenly as the answer came to me.

"Yes," the queen said, giving me a pleased smile.

"I hadn't . . . hadn't realized Thorny was a sorcerer," I admitted. "But I guess it makes sense since you're a fairy."

Queen Rose smiled. "Yes. Most fairies have daughters, but we do have sons on occasion."

"You didn't tell him he's a sorcerer, did you?"

"No, I didn't. But he might have suspected it anyway."

"You said he's not dead," Poppy ventured. "So what is he then?"

Queen Rose seemed almost irked, though I wasn't sure why, but she quickly smoothed her features over. "His spirit has been wrenched from his body."

I frowned and ventured, "A malediction?"

The queen nodded.

"Then that means someone must've sacrificed something dear to curse him," I said, my worry growing once again. "We're lucky he's not dead."

"So if his spirit has been wrenched from his body, where is it?" Poppy asked.

"He must be at Silverthorn," I said, struck once again by an answer. "That's a faelanx. Spirits are drawn there. His probably was, too."

The redheaded fairy smiled. "Very good, Rapunzel. Now, we should probably hurry. The longer a spirit is away from its body, the harder it is to reunite them.

Spirits become . . . disassociated from themselves."

"How long does he have?" I asked.

The queen must have heard the panic in my voice, as she assured me, "Don't worry. We should be able to reach Thorny in time. I only meant that we shouldn't dawdle."

"All right," I said. "I'm going to go find the other horses. Hopefully, they haven't gone far."

"I'll go with you," Poppy said.

It took us several minutes to find Phoenix and Luna, who were both unnerved by their recent experience, but at last we returned, holding their leads.

Queen Rose was sitting on the ground, her son's head in her lap. I watched her stroke his hair for a moment—noting once again the love on her face— before I cleared my throat. "Your Majesty, do . . . do you want to ride Thorny's horse?"

Queen Rose looked at Phoenix. "No, I think we'll need him to carry my son's body. I've had no problems following you as a deer—that form will be fine for me." She looked over at Slate, who appeared somewhat on edge, and she asked him, "Wolf, may I take my son's body so I can try to reunite it with his soul?"

Slate stared at her, and I thought for a moment he was going to refuse her request. But then he rose and took a few steps away, though his gaze on Thorny remained unfaltering.

Poppy and I helped Queen Rose lift the prince's body, which was surprisingly heavy, up onto Phoenix's back. We secured him to the saddle with some rope while Slate continued to watch. When we were done, I stared at Thorny's limp body with my brow furrowed.

He looked so uncomfortable.

As I stood there chewing on my lip, his mother told me kindly, "Don't worry. He won't feel anything."

I gave a slow nod, though I wasn't sure I believed her, and I took a brief moment to really *look* at her, which I had been too awed to do when I first met her at Silverthorn.

Though she was a remarkable beauty, as anyone would expect a fairy to be, I thought her green eyes were her most striking characteristic. There was great intelligence there, to be certain, but there was also a sense of deep sorrow that gave her face a haunting quality. Though her form was small, she did not appear short, and her figure was nicely emphasized by the cut of the white dress she wore. The fact that her long red hair was unadorned and unconfined simply lent a wildness to her image that seemed fitting for a queen who had left her son and husband behind to live her life on her own terms. I could understand why Thorny would be upset with her for leaving, but at the same time, it was admirable that she had mustered the strength to part with the terrible sort of man she had married.

Granted, I had little to judge the king on save the grumbles of the people and what little I had seen of him when he was holding a gun to Thorny's head, but I felt I could trust the judgment of both Thorny and his mother in this instance.

"You really think we can save him?" I asked her, almost fearful of the answer.

But she answered with confidence: "I do. Now, let's find a stream so we can wash everyone's wounds." And then she transformed into a red deer and began to move forward, obviously meaning to lead the way.

Poppy looked at me, but I simply shrugged at her. Then I spurred Luna on to follow the small form before us.

It was a bit disconcerting the way Thorny's mother could talk while in deer form, but her son had been able to speak as a wolf, and it hadn't taken me too long to become accustomed to that. But what made it even stranger was the knowledge that I was traveling with the long-lost Queen Rose, a woman everyone had presumed dead. When I had begun to consider Thorny a friend of sorts, I'd had no idea that he was actually a prince. If I *had* known, things might have turned out very differently.

Since I *was* aware of his mother's true identity, it was hard to talk to her. It didn't help that she had little inclination to talk, which was probably due to the worry she felt for her son in spite of the brave face she was putting on.

"Your Maj—umm, Rose," I managed at last sometime after we had washed our wounds and started traveling again, "am I a fairy?"

The red doe near me halted mid-step, and I brought Luna to a stop.

"Yes," she said, "you are. I knew your real mother, though she died a few years after you were born. She was a fairy, too, and she gave you to me for safekeeping. My hands were too full with Thorny for me to take care of you, too. The sons of fairies tend to

147

be handfuls even as babies."

I was filled with questions, and I spoke some of them out loud in a sort of rush: "Who was my real mother? Why did she send me away? And why did my adopted parents believe that lamb's lettuce could help them have a child?"

The deer looked away. "I will tell you more about your real parents at another time. As for rapunzel, well, though fairies usually try to quell any stories concerning its . . . properties, still some tales persist about it, many of them erroneous."

"And what does it really do?" I asked.

"Let's just say some call it Fairy's Bane and leave it at that."

I felt dissatisfied—there was so much I wanted to know—but I could tell she didn't want to speak any more on those subjects. We walked on for a few more minutes, the pressure inside me building, and I finally blurted, "I think I can talk to animals."

Queen Rose paused and looked back at Poppy, whose horse was behind Luna and Phoenix. "Can you speak to animals, too?" she asked my stepsister.

Surprised, I twisted my neck and saw Poppy flush. *She* was a fairy?

"I can," she admitted, "but I prefer birds over other animals."

I remembered how when we were wealthy she'd had an assortment of songbirds. I had assumed she simply enjoyed the noises they made, but it had apparently been more than that.

"My mother always discourages most of my abilities," she said, "because she is usually too busy with Nettle. But she has always thought talking to animals was a useful skill for me to learn." She paused and then said with some heat, "You're the fairy who cursed us, aren't you?"

I looked at the red doe's fine muzzle and dark eyes, trying to read her expression. I had known the instant I saw Queen Rose's human form at Silverthorn that she was the one who had stripped my family of our wealth. But with everything that had happened, I hadn't thought it worthwhile to brood over the issue, especially since I still felt guilty over her treatment at my family's hands.

"The words of you and your family brought that calamity down on your heads," the queen said softly. "I sacrificed nothing to set those events in motion."

There was a tense silence in the air that I finally broke by saying, "Can you teach me how to hear animals' thoughts?" It was off-subject, perhaps, but there had been something in that quiet that had felt almost murderous.

"Animals' thoughts aren't like our own," answered the queen, looking at me. "You can get impressions from them that your brain will turn into words, but they think best in images. However, they usually do not have any trouble understanding fairies whose communication skills are strong enough. My abilities, unfortunately, aren't very great. I know enough to get you started, but maybe you'd be better off learning from Poppy."

I looked at my stepsister, and she shrugged.

"I don't mind teaching you," she said.

Poppy brought Prince up beside Luna, and while Queen Rose walked behind Phoenix, Poppy began to give me a lesson on speaking with animals.

"You're best off starting with images," Poppy said. "As it becomes more intuitive, you'll get better with imparting your meaning through sentences. Try visualizing something and *pushing* it toward Luna."

I frowned—that was certainly easier said than done—but I tried to picture something in my head, only to have no luck forming a significant image. I looked at Poppy helplessly. "I can't think of anything. I'm coming up blank."

"Then go ahead and try words," Poppy said. "Just push pictures alongside them."

I nodded and then leaned down to whisper to Luna. "My father's dead, Luna, and now Thorny will be, too, if we can't help him." Tears pricked at my eyes.

An image of an apple formed in my mind, and I sat back in surprise. Was she trying to comfort me?

Poppy looked at me. "Did you get something?"

"Yeah," I said.

"How about Prince and I give you some space? Just keep at it, and it will get easier."

So I began talking to Luna, telling her everything on my mind. It became easier and easier to understand Luna's responses, and before long, I was having an actual conversation with her. Granted, it wasn't a normal conversation, but we *were* communicating.

It's hard to describe how learning to speak with animals affected me. Before I had unlocked this part of myself, it was like I had been in a room with no doors and windows, and I hadn't even known about the existence of such things, yet I had felt confined anyway. And then a hidden door had opened, and I suddenly felt free.

Luna and I had so much to tell each other, and I realized her understanding was greater than I had given her credit for. She told me she was sorry about my sire's death and worried about the wolf-boy, and she expressed her confusion as to why we were doing all this journeying in the first place. I explained what I could, and as I did, I realized how scared I was that Thorny would not be saved in spite of our efforts.

"What if this doesn't work, Luna?" I whispered, leaning forward in the saddle and pressing my cheek against her velvety neck. "What will I do then?" Never mind that I hadn't intended to stay with Thorny. Now, I couldn't see myself living without him. He had become too ingrained in my life. Thorny and his fantasizing and his princely pomposity had come to mean a lot to me.

"*It will*," the horse assured me. "*The wolf-boy is strong. He will make it through this.*"

I smiled at her confidence and then looked over at Queen Rose, who suddenly seemed so petite in deer form. "You know," I said to the queen, "even if all I could ever do was talk to animals, I think that's all I need in terms of powers."

I caught a mental image of oats and galloping from Luna and knew she was pleased.

"I'm glad to hear you have that attitude," said Queen Rose. "Many fairies lust after the powers of others or despair over their own limits. It's impossible for such a fairy to find happiness."

I stroked Luna's neck. "I guess some people are always determined to be unhappy."

"It's surprising how many of us strive to create our own unhappiness," agreed Queen Rose. "The harder we try to pursue happiness, the higher its wings take it."

"I guess true happiness is in the here and now."

"Yes," the other woman said, moving her gaze to look at the limp body of her son. "But who among us is ever happy with the here and now?"

Looking at Thorny and feeling my own heart ache, it was hard to disagree with her.

CHAPTER 14:
IN CORPOREAL

Our journey to Silverthorn was relatively uneventful. Now that Poppy and I understood more about how to avoid bandits and redcaps, perhaps that was part of it. But I suspected it was mostly due to Queen Rose.

I wasn't sure if she had spent a long time wandering the woods of her kingdom or what, but she seemed to know the safest paths to take and where it was best to camp for the night. Since she was a queen, I didn't feel it was my place to question her, but I did wonder about how smoothly everything was going.

When we at last reached Silverthorn, we halted in front of the fountain. I looked up at the tier where my rose had once stood, thinking of my father's descriptions of the flower standing there, an image of perfect beauty, and I remembered with a pang of sadness that it was buried by the barn at my stepmother's house.

"What now?" Poppy asked.

"Look around for a—a glowing orb," Queen Rose said. "Perhaps you've heard of a will-o'-the-wisp? That's a spirit being drawn to a faelanx—it gives off a sort of energy as it travels. The reason people become lost when they follow such 'wisps' is that the spirit takes them down fairy paths they aren't supposed to travel. So they become lost until a fairy notices and takes pity on them."

I didn't see anything like what she was talking about, though, and I said: "The servants here were always invisible to me. Do you really think we'll be able to see Thorny?"

She frowned. "I'm hoping his sorcerer energy might still be strong enough that such will be the case. He—" She cut off as Slate suddenly bolted away.

I kicked Luna's sides, and we galloped after the wolf as I shouted at Poppy to stay behind with Thorny's body. But when Slate disappeared into the Rose Maze, I dismounted and went after him on foot. Queen Rose—as a deer—was hot on the wolf's tail.

I had been in the Rose Maze several times without getting any better at navigating it. Yet this time, either my fairy magic or my powers of recall were hard at work, as I didn't even hit one dead end. Though thorns pulled at my clothes due to my haste-induced clumsiness, I ignored their pinpricks and continued forward.

I turned a corner and jolted to a stop to keep from

running into the red deer standing there. Queen Rose was staring at Slate and didn't turn her head at my approach, though her ears twitched at the sound of me behind her.

"Elle?" a voice said.

I looked around, unable to see any glowing orbs, and said, "Umm, Thorny?"

"The wolf," he said.

I looked at Slate and saw he had his tongue lolling out in an undignified fashion.

Then it hit me. "Wait, you aren't actually *inside* Slate, are you?"

"Yeah," the wolf (*Thorny*, now?) said. "I am. I'm not quite sure how it happened."

"Your soul-brother wanted to help you," Queen Rose said. "Is he still in there?"

"Yeah," Thorny said. "He's a sort of subdued presence in here. It's pretty weird, actually."

The queen turned away. "Well, enough of this. Let's see if we can get you back to your *real* body."

I followed both deer and wolf, feeling like this was something out of a book. But instead of being a heroine, I was just some confused girl who never knew what life was going to throw at her next.

"You mind telling me what you're doing here, *Mother*?" Thorny said, his tone somewhere between irked and curious.

"I've been following you to make sure you didn't get killed."

"I knew someone was following us!" I exclaimed. Those flashes of red that I had seen weren't imaginary!

"Yes, well, keeping an eye on the lot of you isn't easy work," Queen Rose said. "If that wolf-friend of

155

yours had been a few seconds later in arriving, Thorny, I would have jumped in that river and saved you myself."

"If you'd been a few seconds later, I *would've* died," said Thorny, but without any real venom. "You sure did a great job of protecting me from the bandits."

"Captain Crestwood never would've actually killed you," she said dismissively.

Thorny stopped walking, in part, perhaps, because he had led us to a dead end with a particularly pretty rose topiary of a wolf that I had never noticed before. "You mean you know him?"

"I wouldn't say that exactly—just that I've played a bit of a hand in his current state," said the queen evasively.

"I should know not to expect a straight answer from you," Thorny grumbled. He led us away from the dead end and back to the proper path, only to pause and turn his silver head toward me. "Have you been all right, Elle?"

Slate's body was a lot smaller than Thorny's had been when his mother turned him into a wolf, and I thought it made him look a little vulnerable. Strangely, I had never really had that impression when it was just Slate in there. But rather than dwell on it, I gave him a small smile and told him, "Yes, Thorny."

He turned and looked at his mother. "Can you give us a few minutes?"

She nodded and walked away with that dignity that somehow seems an intrinsic part of deer body movements. I watched her briefly before focusing my attention on Thorny.

He sat and gazed up at me. "I've been worried

about you."

"You've been worried about *me*?" I exclaimed. "You were the one that got torn from your body!"

He gave me a wolfish grin. "I know. But it really hasn't been too bad here—I've been able to communicate with the Invis since I'm part of the spirit world now."

"You have?" I said in surprise. I had only been able to understand what the invisible servants wanted through their manipulations of water, wind, and fire. "What are they like?"

"Some of them are a big pain in the butt," he said, only to cry out "ow!" as a sudden gust of wind picked up a pebble and knocked him in the head with it. Glaring at the offending rock, he added, "But I guess most of them are all right." He looked down at the ground. "They told me I'm a sorcerer."

"I heard that, too," I said, watching as he looked up in surprise. "Your mother told me."

He let out a huff of air. "I should've known, I guess—I mean, my mother's a fairy. It seems only logical that magic-users would beget magic-users."

I hesitated briefly and then admitted, "I'm a fairy, too."

"Did my mother tell you that?"

"Yeah," I answered, looking down at my hands. Though being a fairy wasn't necessarily a bad thing, I felt sort of ashamed, like I had been ignoring a part of myself.

"Guess I shouldn't be surprised she told you. It sounds like my mother's got a big mouth lately."

"But you aren't surprised that I *am* a fairy," I noted. "How long have you known? Have you known since

Silverthorn and just never told me?"

"No," he said, tilting his head at me. I must have sounded upset, and the thought that he had kept something so big from me certainly didn't make me happy. "I just thought the rat thing kind of leaned that way."

I let out a dry chuckle. "I guess I tried really hard to ignore that incident, didn't I?"

"The word 'denial' pretty much sums it up," he agreed.

I dropped down to his level and looked in his eyes. "I really *am* glad you aren't dead, Thorny."

"So am I," he said wryly.

I gave him a hug and squeezed him tightly. "I kept trying not to think about what happened to you. Your mom and the whole fairy thing helped, but deep down, I was really scared."

He brought a paw up and made an effort to pat my back. "You don't need to worry. The Invis have been taking care of me. They've taught me a bit about accessing my powers—after all, spirits like them help make magic possible. They thought maybe if I became strong enough in the basic elemental forces, I could break free of Silverthorn, even if it *is* a strong faelanx."

I pulled away from him. "Are the spirits like . . . the ghosts of humans?"

"I don't know," he said with a shrug of his furry shoulders. "They don't seem to know either. If they *were* humans, they can't remember who they once were. I think maybe they're the spirits of plants and animals—or maybe just some kind of special energy created by the elements they're associated with."

I got to my feet. "Well, whatever they are, I'm glad

they've been here for you."

"So am I."

We walked back to where the horses were. Poppy and deer-Rose were standing beside them, and they watched us approach.

"Thorny," said Poppy in relief. "I'm so glad you're alive." She looked as if she wanted to approach but feared his new form.

"I've been getting that a lot lately," the prince said dryly. Then he looked at his mother expectantly and sat down. "So . . . we've got a lot to talk about."

Queen Rose laughed. "I guess I can't deny that."

"How about we start with what happened to me?" Thorny suggested.

"Well, to put it simply, you were cursed by a bad fairy."

"A bad fairy?" he repeated.

"A fairy's magical abilities, long life, and beauty are all meant to advance the course of love for herself and others," Queen Rose explained. "When a fairy wants to do something to hurt others, she must sacrifice something, just as Rapunzel's stepmother made a sacrifice to curse you."

I took a step forward. "Wait—what do you mean, my stepmother?"

"My mother is not a bad fairy," said Poppy in a low voice. I tended to agree with her. Iris wasn't exactly a kind person, but she was no murderer.

"I would believe it," said Thorny flatly. "I had no interest in Nettle, and she hated you, Elle. She was the one who sent that huntsman after you."

"She couldn't afford to pay Mr. Treeson," I protested.

159

"I think she'd be willing to give up a few pretty baubles to wreak vengeance on the world," Thorny said. He turned to Poppy. "I guess I shouldn't be surprised that you have fairy blood. I thought you played with birds a little too much for your own good."

Poppy flushed, and I looked at Thorny in surprise. I had honestly thought he didn't pay enough attention to my stepsister to notice something like that.

Thorny then addressed his mother: "There's one question I want to ask you . . . . Do you see a happily ever after in our futures, or should we just give up and go home now?"

The red deer's dark eyes narrowed. "My ability to see the future doesn't work quite like that."

"Then how does it work?"

The queen sighed. "Imagine a great river. There are many twists and turns, and sometimes the path branches out in more than one direction. You may become so focused on a nearby rapid that you don't notice the fork ahead. Yet if you leap ahead along the course, you may also be missing an important branch. You have to chart a path and plan the variables—but even while you do that, you don't know whether everything will come to pass. All you can do is hope that the actions you take will lead to one of the pleasant paths."

"Sounds like you shouldn't even bother to me," muttered Thorny.

"It does tend to work better with events that are weeks away rather than years," said the queen mildly.

"And what about this whole sorcerer thing?" Thorny asked. "Why have you been keeping it from me?"

"You must understand that magical blood in a man is much more chaotic than that in a woman. It's harder for him to control his powers, and his strengths tend to mostly be along the lines of destructive magic like fire. It's this wildness in a man's blood that usually calls a soul-brother to him—an animal of a species whose soul is somehow similar to his own."

"And fairies don't have that?"

"No. While we may have our preferences, we tend to appeal to all kinds of animals."

"Well," said Thorny, "while I enjoy talking with you and all, I think it would be more enjoyable if I could do it from *my* body."

Taking the hint, Poppy and human-Rose and I all managed to lift his body off Phoenix after removing the bonds that were holding it in place. Thorny approached his body, and I held my breath.

CHAPTER 15:
DREAMS

horny stared down at his body. "So, uh, what am I supposed to do exactly?"

Queen Rose laughed. "I haven't exactly been disembodied myself before, you know. But I would start by trying to focus on your body—how everything feels and smells and sounds different from the body you're presently in."

"All right," he said. He put his large paws on the chest of his motionless body. Then he tucked in his chin and closed his eyes.

I couldn't visually see his efforts, but I was able to witness the results of them. Suddenly, the wolf staggered off and away from Thorny's body.

"Battling basilisks!" exclaimed wolf-Thorny. "Some

162

kind of barrier threw me back."

Queen Rose frowned. "I was worried it might be too strong for you to do it on your own. Girls, come here!"

Poppy and I moved toward her as requested.

"Kneel and touch both the wolf's body and Thorny's," instructed the queen.

"Umm, do we really have to touch the wolf?" Poppy asked.

Queen Rose pursed her lips in frustration. "Right now, that wolf is my *son*, child, and if this works, the last thing that wolf will be thinking about when Thorny is out of his head is how to go about biting your ankles."

Poppy flushed, but she moved closer and kneeled without another word. I joined her and the queen in touching the wolf's head and Thorny's human head.

"Now, concentrate, girls," instructed Queen Rose.

"I'm not a *'girl,'*" muttered Poppy in irritation, but the queen ignored her.

"Think of Thorny's . . . whole essence, if you will," Queen Rose said. "Think of how he is mentally and how he is supposed to be physically. Imagine drawing the two together, merging them as one."

I did as she said, thinking of how I saw Thorny. He was a bit roguish, perhaps, and even beastly at times, but he was also fanciful and caring, one-minded and stubborn. I thought of how cruel Fate had been to him, giving him something terrible in one hand to outweigh the silver spoon held in the other. I thought of how his mind and body needed to be connected once more . . . of drawing the former to the latter.

And then it was suddenly as if I had been pushed. I

was flung onto my back and stared upward in confusion for a few seconds before sitting up with a groan. I watched as Poppy and Queen Rose did the same.

"What was that?" Poppy asked, placing a hand on her back with a wince.

Queen Rose sighed. "The curse was too powerful for even the three of us to overcome. We need to go to a place with more power."

"And where's that?" Thorny asked none-too-happily.

The queen smiled. "The place that was your goal all along—Lake Avalon."

"What do you hope to find there? Doesn't Silverthorn have enough power?" I asked. I had never intended to go to the lake—and if even half what that man Linden said was true, it was going to be a rough and perilous journey.

"Silverthorn's magic is too dispersed," said the queen dismissively, waving a hand in the air. "The lake will be smaller than the grounds of Silverthorn, and water has an amazing capacity for retaining magic. Since it is home to the sword—and the magical keeper that resides there—I think we need only dip him in the water. If that doesn't work, perhaps we can use the sword itself."

"You don't actually believe that story about the sword," I said skeptically, only to cover my mouth in horror. Had I actually just talked like that to a queen? "And aren't the lake waters supposed to be dangerous?" I added as I lowered my hand, hoping she wouldn't be offended.

But the redheaded beauty just gave me a half-smile.

"Of course I believe that story. After all, I knew the last queen. She had to get in her position somehow, didn't she? And I wouldn't believe that nonsense about the lake water."

"I don't suppose you've got any tips on how I might try to magick my way out of this body?" asked Thorny.

His mother shook her head. "Sorcerer blood is too chaotic for me to even begin to know how to coach you. It tends toward destruction so much that I suspect even a highly skilled sorcerer wouldn't be able to use gentle means to break the curse that's been put on you. No, the best method is going to be finding the lake."

"Fine," grumbled Thorny. "It's where we meant to go anyway."

I looked down at my hands. Actually, that was where *he* had meant to go. I had intended only to travel to Airland. But now, I had no other choice. I had to make sure Thorny's spirit got back inside his body.

"Now," said Queen Rose, "let us stay here and get a fresh start in the morning. I'm sure we could all use some sustenance and a good night's rest."

Poppy glanced at Thorny, as if she wanted to say something, but then she turned and followed the queen away.

And then, just like that, Thorny and I were left alone with the horses.

"Invis," said the wolf-prince, "can you take care of our mounts? And . . . uh . . . put my body in the bed in my room?"

A soft breeze brushed past my cheek, and I knew it was the invisible servants' sign of agreement.

Thorny and I walked slowly toward the castle, and I thought of the sheep enclosure. "I miss Soleil and Étoile," I told him.

"Don't worry about those sheep of yours. I made sure they're being taken care of."

"I know," I said, giving him a sideways smile. "But I still miss them. I bet Étoile has already grown a lot."

"If you're worried they'll forget you, don't," said Thorny. "I'm sure both sheep would follow you to Airland and back if you asked them."

I laughed at that, thinking of what a sight we would have made with two sheep traipsing around the kingdom with us. We already made a strange enough group as it was. "Well, I'm glad they're safe. I'm not sure they would've enjoyed land-pirates and hungry dwarves."

Thorny shook his head. "Yeah, I don't think they would have. Sheep prefer things nice and boring."

I rolled my eyes and gave him a light kick with my leg.

"Hey!" he protested.

I just grinned at him and started running.

He followed me, yelling, "Elle! Not again!"

I went to *his* room rather than my own, and I was out of breath by the time I got there. The invisible spirits had evidently carried Thorny's body ahead of us without me noticing, as it was lying there on the bed. I stood in the doorway, looking at it.

"I told you not to run when there's a wolf near," grumbled Thorny, coming up behind me. He stared at the bed for a minute before commenting, "You know, it's kind of weird looking at myself like this."

I turned and dropped to my knees and threw my

arms around his furry body. "I'm sorry, Thorny," I whispered. "I'm sorry for fighting with you and getting you into this mess."

"I'm sorry for fighting, too," he said, putting his chin on my back. "But you don't have to apologize for me being ripped from my body. Your stepmother did that, not you."

I pulled away and looked into those two lupine orbs. Though Slate's body was very different from the one that Thorny had possessed when his mother turned him into a wolf, still I could see a flicker of Thorny in those wolfish eyes. "But that's just it," I said. "If it really was my stepmother, she wouldn't have done this if not for her hatred of me."

The wolf's head shook vigorously from side to side. "No, she was upset that I didn't want anything to do with Nettle . . . and she probably found out somehow that Treeson didn't kill you. Maybe he admitted it. She probably figured killing me was a good way to punish us both."

I thought back to the enchanted looking-glass. If Iris *had* sent Birch Treeson to kill me, I knew how she had found out I was alive. Yet though it all seemed logical, I had a hard time believing Iris would actually resort to murder to get her way.

I stood and walked over to the bed. Looking down, I touched Thorny's limp hand. It was dirty from travel; the nails weren't well-groomed anymore, and there were even a few scratches to be seen. It didn't look like a prince's hand—there wasn't a signet ring or anything else to make it more visually appealing. But all that made it even more beautiful to me.

He had been foregoing much of the pomp and

pleasure of his station to go on a dangerous quest for my sake. And now I had to do the last leg of that quest for *his* sake.

I gently squeezed his fingers and then looked back at the wolf staring questioningly at me. "Whatever it was, Thorny, I will do my best to try to fix it. After all, you can't just leave a friend's side, remember? Even if he does want to eat off your plate."

"Thank you, Elle," he said softly.

I turned back to the bed, gazing at that handsome face, thinking of all he had done for me and what he was willing to do, and I felt my heart swell. "Maybe when you . . . when you get your body back, you can give me my . . . my first real kiss." I could feel my cheeks burning.

He tilted his furry head a little, and I thought there was a twinkle in his eyes as he said, "I'd like that. Your lips have been calling to me for a while now."

My cheeks felt like they were on fire, and all I could do was look away from him and say, "Thorny . . ."

Even though he was in a wolf's body, there was no mistaking the smugness of that grin.

That night, I had a dream. I was sitting with Thorny—who was in human form—at the fountain in front of the Silverthorn castle. I was incredibly dirty, like I had been trampled on, but the prince was staring at me intently.

It was nighttime, and the moon cast down a pale light onto our surroundings. Thorny's expression was soft and loving, and I felt I should look away, but I couldn't. He reached over and took my hand, and despite the dirt caked on it, he kissed it.

"I need to clean the fireplace," I said, standing and pulling away from him, but he grabbed me and pressed me against him.

"No, you don't," he murmured. And then he kissed me.

I tried to tell myself I still had to tend to the fireplace, but then I lost myself in Thorny. His hands were on my back, but one moved to rub my arm, and I retreated from his mouth and placed my hands on his chest. I stared up at his eyes, which were dark with desire, and then he moved to press a line of kisses against my neck.

"Thorny," I said, the word a plea.

He put his forehead against mine and closed his eyes. "I would do anything for you. I would give up my life if it could bring your father back."

I pulled back a little and lifted a hand to touch his cheek. "I wouldn't want you to. You mean too much to me. You care for me even now when I'm covered in dirt."

"No amount of dirt can taint my image of you. Your soul is too beautiful—too pure." He turned away. "So unlike mine."

"Thorny," I began, only to cut off as a flock of sheep approached. "Soleil," I said, crouching, trying to encourage the ewe to come closer. When I looked back, Thorny was gone. I returned my eyes to the sheep, only to frown as they began running away *en masse*.

I turned and saw a big black wolf gazing hungrily at

the flock. It looked like Thorny once had, but I knew it wasn't him.

"You aren't Thorny!" I shouted. "He isn't like this!"

The wolf stared at me, teeth glistening in the moonlight, and then he leaped toward me, and I woke up.

My heart was racing, and I took a moment to look around and orient myself. The rose wind chimes tinkled—the invisible servants' way of telling me everything was all right—and I was able to calm myself. But the dream had felt so real that it was hard to push it out of my head.

I got dressed and went outside, where I stood by the fountain, staring at the water and thinking of my dream.

"Couldn't sleep?" a voice asked suddenly, and I jumped.

Heart pounding, I turned to look at Queen Rose. Though she was in a dressing-gown, she looked radiant. Her thick red hair always seemed as if there was never a strand that wasn't where it was supposed to be, and the pale skin of her face simply served as a pleasing contrast to the rosiness of her cheeks and the redness of her lips. I thought again of how she was the ideal image of a fairy, and I wondered if her beauty had set her apart when she was young as mine had.

"Yeah," I answered. "I had a dream that just . . . felt so real."

"Was Thorny in it?"

I flushed. I wanted to deny it, but she would probably know I was lying. "Yes, he was."

"I'm not surprised. He *is* a Dream Invader, after all."

"A Dream Invader?" I repeated, my brow crinkled.

"The term doesn't sound positive, of course, but that isn't surprising since it was coined by fairies. A Dream Invader is a sorcerer with the ability to enter—and even influence—the dreams of others. If they don't know they can do it, then that obviously limits what they are capable of."

"Does Thorny know?"

"No." The woman gave me a slightly guilty smile. "But he dreamed of me a lot when I left his father, and he sometimes entered my dreams accidentally. When I realized what was happening, I used it as a way to check up on him."

I frowned. "That sounds a little underhanded."

"Maybe," Queen Rose said with a shrug. "But I'm his mother. It's my duty to keep an eye on him."

I looked away, uneasy. "I think he should know."

"Whether to tell him or not is up to you. Just remember that he can't unlearn it."

"You don't trust him?"

"I don't trust men," she responded without thinking. But then she tilted her head, as if realizing how what she'd said had sounded, and she smiled at me. "The issue isn't really that I don't trust Thorny. It's just that dreams are personal things. Whether you want to give my son the knowledge that he can invade your dreams is your choice."

"It's my choice even though it affects you as well?"

"Somehow, I think he'll be more interested in your dreams than mine," she said with a laugh.

I could feel my cheeks turn red in embarrassment. To distract her, I asked, "If he can have such control over dreams, then why didn't he remember his dreams as a wolf?"

"Magic can be a little finicky," she told me. "When a body is forced to take a different form, its magic abilities are repressed. Voluntary transformations allow for abilities to remain usable—and even allow for pesky little details like clothes disappearing and reappearing. While Thorny didn't voluntarily wrench his spirit from his body, he *did* voluntarily enter Slate's body. Furthermore, his spirit's resistance to the true intent of the spell appears to have allowed his abilities to remain freely associated with his spirit—which is why he was able to learn from the elemental spirits here." She smiled and patted me on the shoulder. "I think that's enough talking for one night. I'm going to try to get some rest. You should do the same."

I turned toward the fountain, listening to the rustle of her clothes as she walked away. I had to admit that the thought of Thorny entering my dreams was a little frightening. But I felt like my sense of morality was becoming a little slippery lately. Hiding my true motives for traveling with Thorny had been the start of it. And then I had agreed to steal from thieves, which was admittedly a gray area when it came to morality. What I needed was to try to clean my slate. I would tell Thorny my original motives for traveling with him and let him know about his dream abilities. That would help my conscience.

CHAPTER 16:
THE WHITE STAG

In the morning, I woke up early. Apart from the one that had woken me up before my talk with Queen Rose, I couldn't remember any of my dreams, so I figured Thorny hadn't been in my head again. I dressed with the assistance of the invisible servants, smiling at the sound of the wind chimes tinkling together, and then I hurried down the tower stairs and went to stand in front of Thorny's room. I knocked loudly and waited.

The door opened, and I looked down at a sleepy wolf. Thorny yawned and then said, "G'morning."

My resolve faltered, but I made myself push on. "I learned something about your sorcerer abilities that I think you should know."

He blinked a few times. "All right. What did you learn?"

Quickly, I told him everything his mother had said about Dream Invaders, rushing through the explanation in hopes that he might not consider the fact that he could spy on *my* dreams. Of course, my hope was in vain.

"You mean I can peek into your head to see if you're dreaming about me?" he asked with a glint in his eye.

I let out a long-suffering sigh. "I don't know exactly how it works. But I would hope you wouldn't do that."

"And I guess my mother told you all this?" The question was spoken casually, but I thought I saw his black nostrils flare.

"Yeah, she did."

He narrowed his eyes and asked with strained patience: "And she never saw fit to tell me this herself *why*?"

I shook my head. "You aren't thinking about how scary it is to have someone poking around in your dreams because *you're* the one who's going to be snooping. But for whatever reason, your mother wants to keep her agenda hidden. You should know that better than anyone."

He growled a little beneath his breath. "Isn't that the truth. If she wasn't my mother, I'd probably throttle her. I'm sick of all this deception and hidden motive stuff. Everyone needs to start waving a little more honesty around."

I picked at my sleeve uncomfortably. "Thorny, there's something else I want to tell you."

His ears went back. "What?"

"I didn't come on this quest of yours to become queen. I came because I wanted to start a new life in Airland."

"A new life?" he repeated slowly.

I looked down and suppressed the urge to kick the floor. "Yeah, a new life. I didn't believe in your legend, and I told you why I couldn't become your wife—how I didn't want to be disrespected by the people. I—"

He interrupted me. "I've been thinking about that, Elle. I wonder if maybe a lot of that talk about my mother was based on the way my father treated her. I think he wanted a trophy wife and didn't want her to show her strength. A flower that is smothered loses its appeal—maybe that's what happened." He stood and put his paws in my hands, presumably so he could see my face better.

I ignored the slight discomfort of his claws pressing into my palms and looked into his lupine eyes, thinking of the flicker of Thorny that I could see there. It was strange to imagine a human existing in a wolf's body. Holding his paws certainly wasn't like holding hands. The pads on their bottoms were rough, and the claws, while not very sharp, were thick and even a little frightening.

"Maybe you're right," I said. "But I'm still scared. I know the Landdish people might appreciate a fairy queen, but can the Magnolian people also appreciate one?"

He tilted his head. "I think they can, Elle. When they see how much I care for you, they can't help but respect you. And we'll be honest with them. I *want* them to know just how strong you are." He exhaled heavily and dropped his forelegs to the floor, and I found myself missing his warmth. "But I have to admit that my motives for this quest weren't really to make you queen. I thought if you could grow to know the human me better, then maybe there would be a chance that you could grow to love me. Because I love you, Elle."

He had turned his head away in vulnerability; he was, after all, bearing his soul to me. I crouched down beside him. "Thorny—"

"Elle?" said a voice behind me, making me jump.

I stood and turned around to look at Poppy, hoping my cheeks weren't pink. "Yes?"

"Queen Rose said to tell you it's time to leave."

"All right," I said. I looked back at the wolf-prince. "We'll talk later, all right?"

But he didn't respond; he just started barking orders about his body to the Invis, who promptly doused him with water. "I ought to bite you all in half," he growled.

I chuckled and left the room. But those words—"I love you, Elle"—echoed in my head.

We rode our horses into the forest, but once we got beyond Silverthorn's magical influence, a familiar man stepped out of the trees.

"You two ladies are looking well-rested," commented Birch Treeson darkly. He had a pair of bloody marks on his cheeks that appeared to have been caused by a sword or dagger, and when he saw me looking at them, he said, "My employer somehow found out you were alive and saw fit to punish me with these." He held his forefingers up to point at the wounds. "She sent me once more to do the job. If I fail, it's my head. You really should have gone to Airland, Beauty. But I guess you were too busy picking up an animal entourage." He was looking at wolf-Thorny and deer-Rose now.

"Mr. Treeson—" I began, but he cut me off.

"I'm sorry about your prince. It's honorable of you to hold onto his body, but I do think the buzzards would get more enjoyment out of it." He pulled out his pistol. "You have to understand this isn't personal. Not for me anyway."

Two things happened at once. Thorny leaped in the air at the huntsman, and I raised a hand up and cried out.

There was a puff of smoke, and when it cleared, I saw Thorny entangled with a large stag on a pile of clothes. The deer was as white as snow, except for his antlers, which were a cream color. His eyes were closed, but I could see his white chest moving up and down.

Gingerly, Thorny extricated his legs from the deer's and stood, stepping over the huntsman's gun. "What just happened?"

Queen Rose, who was still in deer form, gestured at me with her head. "Rapunzel turned him into an animal, of course."

"Th-that was me?" I stammered. "I don't know how to do that."

"Evidently, you do," the queen said dryly.

I dismounted Luna and went over to the

unconscious Treeson. "Is he going to be all right?" I asked. Unable to help myself, I reached out and touched the base of one of his antlers. It felt like velvet.

"Why do you care whether he will be all right or not?" demanded Thorny. "He nearly killed you!"

"Why don't you ask him yourself?" suggested Queen Rose, ignoring her son's outburst. She quickly transformed into a human and then reached out to touch the stag's head.

Birch Treeson sprang to life, and I jumped backward. Queen Rose, of course, was a little more dignified in moving out of the way.

"What—?" he said, and then he looked down at his hoofed feet. His eyes widened. "What have you done to me?" He lifted his heavy head with a jerk and took in the presence of Queen Rose. "Your Majesty," he said with a gasp. "Have I died?"

The queen's mouth twisted. "Not yet, though death is no less than what you deserve. Instead of meeting that fate, you have been turned into a white stag—and so the hunter becomes the hunted." She gave him a smile that had a certain dark satisfaction in it.

It took him only a few seconds to realize what a prize he would be to any hunter or huntsman, and then he kneeled in front of the queen. "Please, Your Majesty, you must change me back."

"I am not the one who transformed you," she said.

Treeson turned his head to look at me with his almond deer eyes. "I did wonder if there might be something of the fairy in you, Beauty. Please, release me from this beastly form."

"Only love can break the spell," Queen Rose told

him. "But at least now you are free of your mistress."

"Love," he repeated, his timid voice a far cry from that of the arrogant huntsman he had been moments before. "No, no. Not that."

"You loved once," said the queen gently. "You can love again."

Though he had the face of a deer, Treeson gave Queen Rose a haunted look that I will never forget. And then he turned, and with a flip of his tail, he sprinted off through the trees.

"Will he really ever find love?" I asked, staring after him. "How can someone grow to love a stag?"

"The same way someone can grow to love a wolf," the queen answered. "Silverthorn will accept him now, I suspect. And until he finds that out, he'll get a taste of what it is like to be hunted." She laughed when she saw my disapproving look. "He used to have such a way with animals. It will do him good to be reminded of what their lives are like."

"You said he loved someone once. Who was it?"

She studied me for a moment and then answered: "Your birth-mother."

"Wh-what?" I gasped.

"There will be time enough for explanations later," she said. "Let's begin traveling once more." And then she transformed into a deer and walked forward.

"She can be pretty stinking annoying, can't she?" muttered Thorny as he stepped toward me.

I agreed with him, but I thought her deer ears might pick up whatever I said, so I didn't respond out loud.

With Queen Rose to guide us, the journey to the border between Magnolia and Airland was mostly uneventful. I thought for certain we were going to have trouble when the guards saw Thorny's human body on Phoenix and the suspicious wolf-shaped bulge on Luna's back, but the queen gave them a convincing story about how we were taking our cousin and his faithful canine companion back to their homeland for burial (though I guess the coins she provided might have also helped with the believability of her tale).

When we finally stepped foot in Airland, Thorny looked at me and asked, "Does it feel like home?" He said it half in jest, but I could hear the pain in his voice.

I thought of my father and said, "My dad always said that home isn't a place, but a state where you are happy and with the ones you love."

"Then I guess I'm home," he murmured. He didn't mean for me to hear, but I did, and it made me flush.

"So you really think we can find this lake?" Poppy asked Queen Rose.

"Of course. I *have* been there before."

"You what?" Thorny said. "You've known all along this wasn't a fool's errand and didn't see fit to tell us?"

The queen was amused. "I can't give you all the answers at once, can I?"

"If you've been to the lake, then you must know that the sword could never accept someone from Magnolia as its mistress," I said. I wasn't sure whether I was hoping she would contradict me or hoping she would disabuse Thorny of all notions that I might become queen.

"Actually," said Queen Rose, "the last queen, Queen Avery, wasn't from Airland."

"She wasn't?" said Poppy, who seemed particularly interested.

"No, she wasn't."

"How did you know her?" Thorny asked.

"There's a bit of a story there," Queen Rose said. "Oakhill was seventeen when his father passed away—his mother having already died years before while giving birth to Thorny's uncle—and so Oakhill was pulled away from his educational blacksmithing stint before he reached eighteen. He then had to attend the usual celebratory month of balls, though he couldn't be king yet.

"I was newly in love, and I was devastated when he left to return home to the castle. I thought I was saying goodbye forever. But then I received an invitation to the balls, and I felt there was hope for us yet."

"Of course he didn't bring the invitation to you himself," grumbled Thorny.

Queen Rose crossed her arms, looking slightly irritated at the interruption. "He was too busy for that. *Anyway*, at the first ball, he danced with this beautiful young woman, and I was jealous of the way he laughed with her. I feared he meant to cast me aside for another young beauty. But then Avery noticed the dark looks I directed at her, and she came to me and told me not to worry, for she was in love with a stableboy."

"What was she like?" I asked, curious.

"Though she kept her heritage a secret, she was the very image of what people believe fairies to be. She would flit from here to there, constantly cheerful, laughing and giggling over this or that. Never have I met a kinder person. When Oakhill and I had a terrible fight the next week, she told me that I needed to get away from the castle and go on a grand adventure. I thought she was being a little daft, but I agreed to go with her. She meant to make me queen, for then, she said, I could laugh down my nose at Oakhill, who couldn't even wear his crown until he was twenty-one.

"But when we reached the lake, I failed to retrieve the Arm of Avalon."

"So then you told Avery to try," guessed Poppy.

"Yes," said Queen Rose. "With a giggle, she went to ask for the sword . . . and she was granted it."

"Weren't you upset with her?" Poppy asked.

"Magic isn't something you trifle with. We both knew that. But even still, she tried to give the sword to me. When I refused it, she wanted to toss it back into the water, but I convinced her not to. We both knew she was meant to be the next queen."

I thought of how Queen Avery didn't want the burden of leadership. In some ways, there was great wisdom in that. I thought, too, of the stableboy she had left behind in Magnolia so she could go to the aid of a hurting friend. "And what of the stableboy?" I asked.

"Well," Queen Rose said, looking away, "perhaps I shall tell you more about him a different time."

I was disappointed, but I knew there was no sense in trying to pry more out of her. I looked at Thorny and saw his wolf eyes roll. I pressed my lips together and fought the urge to snicker.

CHAPTER 17:
REGAL BEASTS

irland looked much the same as Magnolia. There were, perhaps, a few more birds, but that was the only noticeable difference. I was, however, impressed when we came to the base of the Peregrine Mountains. Queen Rose readily explained that they were named after the multitude of falcons that built their nests along the north side. She took us along a path between two of the mountains after briefly scoping out the area in bird form. I was beginning to realize how useful her transformation skill was. But I supposed it had its own burdens—surely anyone who could turn into a mouse would be tempted to eavesdrop. Perhaps it was best that only a few fairies had that ability.

The journey along the path between the mountains was uneventful until we reached the craggy area at their base. That was when a chimera reared up from behind a large rock and glared at us.

I had seen pictures of chimeras before, though I had never been certain they really existed. The one before me had the head of a lion, the body of a goat, and the tail of a snake. Furthermore, she was twice the size of Thorny's wolf body. And she looked angry.

"Use your ability to talk to her," encouraged Queen Rose, but all I could do was stand there, frozen, and stare at the beast's glistening teeth as she prepared to pounce.

Thorny leaped at her, and she roared in pain and anger as he sank his teeth into her shoulder. With a jerk of her body, she shook him off. Then she opened her mouth and began to breathe fire.

Somehow, I snapped out of my paralysis—possibly because of Poppy's piercing screams—and called the fire escaping the beast's mouth into my hands. Then I threw it at the chimera's feet, making her flinch backward.

Thorny had been flung so hard that he was struggling to stand, and I let my concern for him fuel my resolve. I made the flames dance in front of the chimera.

With a roar of frustration, she turned away, apparently deciding to retreat elsewhere for easier prey.

When I was certain the chimera was gone, I dismounted Luna and rushed over to Thorny.

"That was a great job, Elle," he said, gritting his teeth as he finally managed to get to his feet.

"No, it wasn't," I snapped. "I was too slow and

almost got you killed. I panicked."

"That's a normal reaction when you face a creature like that for the first time," said Queen Rose soothingly.

"You can't afford to be afraid when someone's life is in danger," I said. "You have to act fast."

Even though he was a wolf, I could tell Thorny was giving me a weird look. "Why would you expect to save everyone?"

"What good are magical powers if you can't help people?" I asked. I took a deep breath, trying to calm myself. "I'm sorry. I guess I'm just . . . I'm tired of feeling helpless. I'm tired of feeling like I can't do any good in this world."

"You have to remember, Rapunzel, that small actions and small kindnesses may mean the world to someone," Queen Rose said. "If you can make even one person happy, doesn't that mean you have accomplished something?"

I thought of my father, who only ever wanted to make people happy. Though he had never done anything big like stop a war or save someone's life, would I ever say that his life hadn't been worth living?

"I guess you're right," I said. "It's just . . . hard."

"Fear is a natural emotion—an instinct, even," she said. "Some of us are meant for flight, and others for fight. You have to decide which for yourself."

But as I thought of Poppy, who was scared of everything, I knew I didn't want to be meant for flight. If I showed the people of Magnolia that I was a proud fairy with a strong desire to help them, wasn't it possible they would accept me as their queen? Couldn't I stand proudly by Thorny's side?

I looked over at Thorny, who was sniffing the air, and I smiled to myself. Maybe my answer didn't have to be "no" the next time he proposed.

"I think we have attracted some other chimeras," he said. "We should probably start moving."

Poppy kicked Prince into action, leading the way.

We managed to bypass the rest of the chimeras—Queen Rose explained that they tended to move slowly, even if they could strike quickly—and we entered the forest surrounding Lake Avalon. "It's called the 'Demon Dogs' Den,'" she said. Despite Thorny's blatant disapproval, she had transformed into a red wolf, explaining that she didn't want to attract predators by smelling like a deer.

We had to lead our horses slowly through the forest because it was a tangled terrain of vines and bushes and rocks. The trees weren't any better. They seemed almost gnarled and twisted—even foreboding, if a tree could be that. Thorny looked as if every hair on his body were standing on end.

"What's wrong?" I asked him. "Do the garms smell that bad?"

"I don't think we should be here," said Poppy, her voice little more than a squeak.

"I've smelled garms before," Thorny said, "but this forest is *filled* with their stench. The whole place is their territory, and I don't know how I'm going to tell when they're nearby."

"Don't worry," said the queen. "Garms always

travel in packs, and unlike wolves, whenever they find suitable prey, they always announce their presence."

No sooner had those words left her mouth than a chorus of howls rang through the air.

"You had to say that," muttered Thorny, crouching into a protective stance.

"Girls," said Queen Rose in a tight voice, "get on the horses. Better to face the possibility of getting thrown off than the certainty of being trampled."

Though I didn't believe Luna would do anything of the sort, I climbed up on her anyway. Then I began talking to the horses calmly. They were uneasy, shifting in place, flaring their nostrils, and flicking their ears.

"*I don't know where they are,*" Luna said, troubled.

"Don't worry," I told her. I was worried enough for us both. It had sounded like the pack was surrounding us.

And then there they were.

The garms stepped lightly out of the trees, like they knew their quarry had nowhere to go. Their fur was a brilliant white, and their eyes were dark pink in color. But their most noticeable feature was their faces, which looked as though they were stained with blood. Their teeth were bared in silent snarls as they stared at us, ready to attack. Compared to this, that chimera had been a kitten. There had to be at least twelve of the vicious dogs.

"Stop!" I told them as one prepared to jump on Thorny. "We are not your enemy or your prey! You must let us pass through here!"

One of the beasts gave the others a signal to back down, and he stepped forward out of the pack. He was the largest, and I knew instantly that he was Alpha.

"*What makes you think you are worthy of walking in the forest we have been protecting our entire lives, pup?*" he asked me.

"Rapunzel?" asked Queen Rose hesitantly.

"I can understand them," I told her, and then I addressed the Alpha again. "What I want isn't to possess the power the Arm of Avalon promises. What I want is to help my friend. He is meant to be in his human body, not that of a wolf."

"*His human body could feed us all tonight,*" the Alpha said, eyeing Thorny's limp form on top of Phoenix.

"But you aren't here to feed," I told him, my heart fluttering. "You are here to protect."

He turned and looked at Queen Rose. "*We know her scent. She has not come here again to try her hand at attaining that which we protect, has she?*"

"No, that's not why she's here. She is already a queen. She is here to support me."

"*And the other pup on the horse? Her fear burns our noses.*"

"They are all with me," I told him.

The Alpha stared at me. "*Would you give up one of your horses for us to spare your lives?*"

"No," I said immediately. "I would not."

"Elle!" cried Poppy. Apparently, she could understand them, too.

"*You are certain?*" asked the Alpha.

"Yes. We have to all stay together."

He licked his red jowls and sighed. "*Very well.*" Then he turned to the pack and spoke with a voice of command. "*They shall move through the forest untouched. They may now be considered under the protection of the Lady of the Lake until they leave the forest.*"

He looked at me and said by way of farewell, "*May your paws forever escape the stone's bite.*" He gave a surprisingly regal bow before moving and leading his pack back through the trees.

I exhaled heavily and looked at Queen Rose.

She seemed to be smiling, though I wasn't as good at reading her wolf-face as I was Thorny's. "I couldn't catch much of that," she said, "but judging by the result, I'd say you did a good job."

"Are all predators that nice?" I asked, frowning.

"Certainly not. Usually, it's just the magical ones meant to guard something for centuries that take on human characteristics."

"You mean those garms are hundreds of years old?" I asked in surprise.

"They're at least that old, if not older," she answered. "I did some research after the last time I was in these woods, and longevity is something garms seem to be blessed with. I've never personally met the garms around Silverthorn because they're in the forest only to protect the castle from those meaning harm. These, it seems, have stricter orders."

"How did you get by them the last time you were here?" Thorny asked.

Queen Rose smiled. "Oh, Avery talked to them just like Rapunzel did. But she was not nearly so firm and even offered to give them baths." Part of her lip quirked upward at the memory.

"You're kidding," Poppy said in horror. "Why would anyone want to touch those things?"

"Some people actually appreciate the canine form," said Thorny, annoyed. "It's just a little blood on their faces."

"I'm sorry, Your Highness, but that was *more* than a little bit of blood," began Poppy.

"It doesn't matter," I said quickly. "Let's just go to the lake to try to reunite Thorny's body and spirit. That's what we're here for, isn't it?"

The two grumbled a bit but agreed. And so we began to travel once more.

CHAPTER 18:
PURIFYING WATERS

Navigating an unfamiliar forest with treacherous undergrowth was a stressful endeavor, but at last we broke out into a beautiful clearing. The grass was bright green and lush, unlike most of the sparse grass in the forest, and the trees at the edge of the clearing had lost that gnarled appearance and instead seemed welcoming. Birds sat in the trees' branches, singing cheerfully, and I caught Poppy staring at them with a smile.

In the center of it all was a pristine lake, the surface undisturbed and looking almost like glass.

Thorny approached the water and stared down at his silver reflection. "So," he said, "what now?"

"I haven't exactly done this part before," said

Queen Rose dryly, "but I think it would be wise to ask permission from the Lady of the Lake before we simply dump a body into the water."

"Do you think she'll answer?" Poppy asked skeptically.

"I guess we're about to find out," said Queen Rose. She changed back into her human form and began unfastening Thorny from Phoenix's saddle.

I dismounted and helped her, feeling suddenly nervous. What were we going to do if this didn't work?

"This is surreal," commented Thorny. "Staring at my body . . . I dunno. I seem kind of big and awkward."

"Well, if you're lucky," his mother said, "you'll be back in that big and awkward body soon." She gestured for me to help her, and I assisted with lifting Thorny's body and placing it in front of the water's edge.

Then Queen Rose spoke. "Lady of the Lake, we ask that you allow us to dip my son's body into your waters in an attempt to restore his soul to its proper casement."

We waited expectantly, but no answer came.

"Does that mean she disapproves?" asked Poppy, somewhat timidly.

Queen Rose pursed her lips. "I don't think so. Thorny, it's probably best if you also go into the water with your body."

"Are we going to dip him completely?" I asked, worried.

Thorny, who was eyeing the water skeptically, jumped when his mother ordered sharply, "Thorny, stand in the water."

He glanced at her and then did as she said, though he grumbled a little about her bossiness.

Ignoring his words, she looked at me and said, "His entire body is cursed, so I do think we need to cover him completely with the lake water. Thorny, the instant we do that, you need to try to jump into your body. I don't think it's a good idea to hold your body underwater any longer than we have to, so you need to take control quickly."

I watched as wolf-Thorny waded deeper into the lake. "This water feels strange," he commented. "It's not what I expected."

Queen Rose looked at me. "Are you ready?"

"Yes," I said.

As one, we hoisted up Thorny's human body and stepped into the lake.

Thorny had not been exaggerating when he said the water felt strange. It was thicker than I expected, and it felt almost abrasive, as if it were scouring away physical and emotional blemishes.

We moved a little deeper to reach a place where we could fully submerge Thorny's human body while still not getting too wet ourselves. Then Queen Rose said, "Now, Rapunzel," and we dunked him.

Almost instantly, Thorny's body turned rigid, and he began struggling in our arms, so we released him.

Thorny sat up in the water, gasping for air, and I dropped to my knees, throwing my arms around him and burying my face in his shoulder. "Thorny," I gasped into his wet clothes.

Though he was still coughing a little, he brought his arms around me and hugged me tightly. When he had recovered more, he murmured, "Elle," and placed a kiss in my hair.

I shivered and hugged him tighter. "I'm so glad you're all right."

"So am I," he said. He pulled back and looked at me, the ghost of a smile on his face as he brought a hand up and pushed a lock of hair out of my eyes. As his hand cupped my cheek, I thought he was going to pull me in for a kiss, but instead, he just dropped his hand and squeezed mine. And then he struggled to get to his feet.

I helped him, and once he was standing, he looked at his mother and Poppy. "Thank you all for your help."

Poppy gave him a shy smile. "We'd do anything for you, Thorny."

Thorny moved unsteadily toward Slate, who had full control of his body again. The wolf now sat on the grass, watching Thorny. He had already shaken off the excess water, and only time would dry him further.

"Thank you, wolf-brother," Thorny said softly. "You can leave if you want. You've already helped me enough."

Slate had an expression on his face that almost seemed like the canine version of a grin. "*Young cubs get into too much trouble by themselves,*" the wolf said. "*I think you may have need of me yet.*"

Thorny laughed, and I found myself smiling, too. When Thorny was happy, his face really lit up.

The prince shook his head, trying to get some of the water out of his hair. Then he began wringing his shirt dry.

Poppy approached him and put a hand on one of his arms, moving it up and down. "You look very handsome wet," she murmured.

Thorny lifted his other hand to remove her hand from his arm delicately . . . and drop it not-so-delicately. "No, I look like a drowned wolf."

She then tried to put her arms around him, and he wiggled out of her grasp while giving her a look of disbelief. Then, clearing his throat, he came closer to his mother and asked, "So how does Elle go about asking for this sword anyway?" When Poppy took a few steps toward him, he held a finger up in warning, as if to tell her: *Don't.*

The queen spread her hands. "Simply ask for it. There isn't a required script."

I felt the squeeze of fear on my heart and said, "Poppy needs to try."

Thorny looked at my stepsister. He wasn't quite able to hide his skepticism—or his disgust. "You want *Poppy* to be queen?"

"I came here for you," I said. "I didn't come here to become queen."

Queen Rose, whose expression seemed almost tight, turned to Poppy. "Do you wish to try?"

Poppy took a deep breath to calm herself. "Yes, I do."

Queen Rose made a sweeping gesture at the lake, and Poppy stepped toward it.

Once she had stopped at the water's edge, she inhaled deeply again, obviously nervous. "Oh, Beautiful Lady," she said, "will you bequeath the Arm of Avalon unto me? I am certain that with such a powerful sword in hand, it will give me the courage I need to be a strong queen. You need not fear for your kingdom while I am at its head."

We all looked at the water expectantly. I wasn't sure what I thought to see there—bubbling, maybe—but nothing happened.

"Could someone have already gotten the sword?" Thorny asked. He was sitting down by the horses and looked tired.

"Thorny, do you want some food?" I asked before his mother could say anything. "It might get your strength back up."

He frowned. "Don't you care about the sword?"

"If that sword is here, it will still be around in five minutes," I told him. I went to Luna and rummaged in one of the saddlebags. I brought out an apple and some dried meat and handed them to Thorny. "That should be a start."

He rolled his eyes and took a bite of the apple. "There. I ate something. Now, ask for that pixie-bit sword before I ask Slate to take a bite out of *you*."

I glanced at the wolf, who gave a big yawn. "*Right,*" I said.

I took a few steps forward, noting Poppy's disappointed expression as I did so. She had really wanted this, and I knew why. It would have been an accomplishment she could hold up to her mother with pride. I had no parent to praise me. Wouldn't it have been better for Poppy to become queen? I certainly didn't deserve it. I still felt stained by my father's death—I should have known how affected he would have been by sending me off in his stead to act as companion for a wolf. I didn't deserve to be queen. Wasn't I meant to be the ashy girl cleaning up the cinders?

I could feel everyone's eyes on me, and I took a

deep breath, staring down at the undisturbed water. "Kind lady, I ask for the Arm of Avalon not because I expect it or deserve it. I ask for it because my companions have helped bring me here. I have never been queen, and I might make a terrible one. I feel soiled by my past. I've made many bad decisions, and I'm certain I'll make many more. But all I can do is ask forgiveness." It felt like I needed to say more, yet I was also sure there was no more I needed to say. The Lady of the Lake would judge me in her own fashion regardless of what words came out of my mouth.

As I looked down at the lake, the glasslike surface broke, and the tip of a sword came through, followed by the rest of the sword and an elegant female hand. Sunlight came down and hit the sword, making it shine so bright I had to shield my eyes for a moment. Then, I looked on in wonder at the smooth-skinned arm that extended upward into the air, fingers curling tighter around the mystical object.

A clear voice without a body rang throughout the clearing, *thrumming* in my ears and making me jump. "Come forward, child. I have chosen you to be the Fairy Queen, for your heart is filled with love. Your mistakes will be forgiven. Come into the water."

I was so mesmerized by this brief glimpse of the Lady of the Lake that I couldn't even turn my head to seek approval from Thorny's mother. I took a few steps forward into the lake and felt that same scouring feeling. I went a little deeper before I was suddenly yanked under.

I began to struggle. I could hear Thorny's muffled voice shout my name. In panic, I opened my eyes.

I felt instantly that they had been cleansed. But all I

could really see was a blinding white light.

"Do not be afraid," the Lady of the Lake told me, her voice kind but filled with strength. "You are the one I have chosen to lead this kingdom. You should rejoice."

I opened my mouth, surprised to find that no water rushed in. And more importantly, I was able to breathe. "Why have you chosen me?"

"Everyone who draws breath has weaknesses, child. Do not castigate yourself. Take strength in the lives of others. Mercy, kindness, love—these are things you know. Do not lose sight of them. Have faith that Good will always prevail."

I wanted to say something more—to ask her questions—but all I could do was lift a hand, scarcely able to resist the impulse that compelled me to do so.

A distinctly swordlike object was pressed into my palm, and as I clenched my fingers around the handle, I was released from whatever force was encompassing me, and I swam swiftly to the surface.

"Elle!" Thorny yelled, breaking free of the grip his mother had on him. He came splashing into the water and embraced me. "Don't you *ever* do that again!"

I was carefully holding the sword out to the side, and as he pulled away, I told him, "I didn't exactly have a choice!"

"Yeah, well, be careful next time," he said grumpily.

I smiled in amusement and looked down at the sword. Despite being submerged in water for years, the blade was unblemished. The handle itself felt molded to my hand, and it was decorated with golden filigree. As I turned it in my hand, I saw a sapphire on one side and a ruby on the other.

"So that's the Arm of Avalon," Thorny said in wonder.

"Water and fire," explained Queen Rose, who noticed me looking at the gemstones. "They signify balance."

"I still don't understand why this was given to me," I said softly.

"I believe it was meant for you," Queen Rose said. "Your parents, after all, were the last queen and king."

"Wh-what?" I gasped, nearly dropping the sword.

"Queen Avery Grayfeather and King Tarragon Grayfeather. Though your mother spent most of her childhood in Magnolia, she was born in Airland and given a Landdish name."

"And my father?" I asked. His name was a blend of names from the two kingdoms.

"In Airland, a husband usually takes his wife's last name. With the ultimate power in the kingdom traditionally being placed primarily on the queen's head, they tend to have more respect for women."

I bit my lip. "If my parents ruled a kingdom, why did they send me away?" Though Gaheris Beauregard was all I could have wanted in a father, it still hurt to know that someone who should have been quite capable of taking care of me had discarded me.

The queen sighed. "It's because of the curse of being a fairy."

CHAPTER 19:
UNSOILED

The curse of being a fairy?" Poppy asked in confusion. She had been quiet since her failure to retrieve the Arm of Avalon, and while she still seemed unhappy, she had been brought out of her sulk by what the queen had told us.

"Well," responded Queen Rose with a slight frown, "it isn't really a definite curse so much as a potential one."

"What do you mean?" Thorny asked, glancing at me. I could see that his protective instinct had been aroused.

"Fairy marriages are more complicated than normal human ones. For a fairy to be truly married, she must perform a blood rite in which she mixes her blood with that of her husband. But this blood rite changes her—it takes away her long life, her magic abilities, and her beauty. Her children still have magic blood, but externally, she has permanently lost that which made her a fairy."

Thorny's face had darkened during her explanation, and he asked her: "What happens if she performs this rite with a sorcerer?"

His mother looked away. "A sorcerer's blood is primal, chaotic. Somehow, it lacks the more love-based components of a fairy's blood. If a fairy does the blood rite with a sorcerer who doesn't have a good heart, she dies, and he absorbs her powers. That's one of the reasons fairies have distrusted sorcerers for centuries."

"What happens if you don't do the blood rite?" Poppy asked.

When Queen Rose looked up, her eyes were filled with pain. "They say that then the marriage becomes cursed. Maybe it's true. Or maybe not doing the blood rite is just a sign of the inevitable bad things to come. For you see, when a fairy doesn't do the blood rite, it's either because of some distrust of her husband or because she wants to retain her beauty or abilities or longevity. Rapunzel, for your mother, it was partly the latter—she felt that fairy characteristics were important to her identity as queen, and she didn't want to give them up. As for myself, I hid the fact that I was a fairy from Oakhill. Avery was strong enough to give up her child to lessen the curse's effects. I was not. Thorny, I'm sorry for that. I know your childhood was filled with unhappiness."

I looked at the prince. His mouth was drawn tight,

and his expression was grim. He said, "This whole time . . ."

"We must go to the Patient Steward," Queen Rose said, changing the subject. "He has safeguarded the throne since your mother died a few years after your birth, Rapunzel."

"You don't think he'll be reluctant to give it to me, do you?" I asked uneasily.

She smiled. "Certainly not. He was the Patient Steward when your mother went to become queen, and he'll be more than happy to give up the throne once again."

"All right," I said. I looked down at the Arm of Avalon. This was too much to believe. I wasn't really becoming queen, was I?

"What should I do since I don't have a scabbard?" I asked.

"Let's wrap it in cloth," suggested Queen Rose.

So we wrapped the sword up in a blanket, and once it was safely tied to my saddle, I mounted my faithful mare. Poppy and Thorny both got up on their horses as well, yet their expressions didn't bear even a hint of happiness for me. Only Queen Rose had a pleasant expression, and the comfort I took in that vanished when she became a deer and I could no longer make out her expression.

My thoughts were a muddled mess, and I was frightened of what was to come. Not to mention I didn't understand why Thorny wasn't gloating or rejoicing over the fact that we had been successful at retrieving the sword.

I began murmuring a little to Luna about my troubles, but all she could send me in return were images of apples and oats, which didn't have quite the effect she wanted.

Queen Rose led us out of the forest, past the craggy mountain bases, and toward Starling, the capital of Airland. Skilled though the queen was at navigating the land and using a bird form to find the best paths, I had a feeling that the garms had something to do with the fact that we didn't run into any more chimeras. But whatever the reason, I was glad for the ease of our travels.

Poppy rose out of her gloom after I tentatively asked if she would like to be one of my attendants when I was queen. Once she began to talk about the types of dresses she would wear and the pet birds she would buy with her allowance, I knew I didn't need to worry about her any longer. Thorny, however, was a different story.

He continued to brood, and though I attempted more than once to determine what was wrong, he kept brushing me off. I finally realized that he would tell me what his issue was when he felt ready, though I was worried that I was no longer finding him in my dreams.

His mother and I talked a lot. She was fairly forthcoming when speaking about my mother the queen, though she skirted around the subject when I asked about my father. Still, I was so happy to learn something that I didn't try to push my luck.

When we finally reached Starling, we were all tired

from days of travel. But I found myself perking up anyway. The architecture in Airland—which I hadn't seen much of before—had a more aesthetically pleasing quality to me than that found in Magnolia. But more noticeable than the style of buildings were their bright colors. Pink, yellow, red, bright blue— these colors and more could be found adorning the exterior of people's homes. In addition, the houses were crowded together and built tall—whether for multiple families or for purely visual reasons, I had no idea.

Poppy's favorite thing was the birds. The Landdish love for birds was evident from the outside of many of the homes. Perches, bird-baths, feeders, and nooks for nests—these were found on buildings in abundance. The air was filled with birdsong, and a variety of avian forms could be seen in and around people's homes and businesses.

Thorny pulled himself out of his brooding long enough to remark, "Just where you want to live. A place where the streets are paved with bird droppings." But in spite of that comment and a few grumbles about leaving Slate behind in the woods, I saw him looking with interest at a tiny thing Poppy informed us was a hummingbird.

Before long, the castle was in plain view. It was a magnificent stone structure, but the gray flags flying high above it somehow lent it a somber feel.

"When it's announced that Rapunzel is to be queen, the flags will be switched to red," Queen Rose told us.

But the grandeur of it all was making me falter. "Your Majesty," I said, forgetting I wasn't supposed to call her that, "how can I be expected to go in there like *this*?" I tugged at my dress, which was grimy and tattered after all we had been through. I had washed it in a few streams, but attempting to clean it had seemed more of a formality than anything.

"Rapunzel," the queen said gently, "surely you realize by now that clothes don't make the woman?"

I wasn't sure if what she had said was really a question or was actually a statement, and I looked down at my dress again. Then I brought my hands up to gaze at them. There was dirt caked beneath my nails, which had been broken and jagged ever since I had left Silverthorn and begun manual labor once more. I could concentrate on the supposed unpleasantness of their appearance . . . or I could think about what the state of those nails represented. They symbolized hard work.

And as for my dress—didn't it symbolize both that work and the long journey I had been on? Shouldn't these tatters and this dirt represent something that wasn't a stain to my soul and physical appearance, but a trophy of my struggles? Why was dirt always to be shunned? The rain that washed the soil from my skin was also the rain that seeped into the dirt and enabled plants to grow. Maybe I had been uprooted from life as I had known it with my beloved father, but hadn't I been finding my own soil, my own water?

When I finally looked into the queen's eyes, I had been taken over by this epiphany, and I felt rooted in the world once more. Had it really been Queen Rose's beauty, as I had believed, that had caused her people to disrespect her? Or had it been more the fact that she had not shown her strength to her people because she had feared the effect it would have on the one she loved?

I glanced at Thorny, who still seemed troubled. I knew he loved me whether I was a fairy or not, and I would gladly give up all that was involved in being a fairy to be with him. I didn't want to hide things from him. And I knew now that I cared too much for him to ever let him go.

"You're right, Your Majesty," I said with a smile. "I'm tired of fretting over my appearance. Let the people of Airland see me as I really am."

"Wonderful," the queen said. "I will remain with the horses out here, but you must enter the castle with pride."

I was nervous, not proud, when I walked up to the castle entrance with the Arm of Avalon resting across my hands. Thorny and Poppy were following me quietly, and I was grateful for their support, yet in some way, I felt alone. What lay ahead had to do with only me, and their presence wouldn't change that.

A pair of guards at the entrance eyed us warily, clenching their rifles, and one said, "You can't come inside the castle with a sword."

"I bear the Arm of Avalon," I said simply. I hoped they couldn't see me trembling.

The guards exchanged a surprised look.

"Very well," said the guard who had spoken before, moving to strap his rifle on his back. "Hand me the blade, and I'll take you to the Patient Steward."

Thorny stepped forward, about to protest handing

over the sword, but I gave him a sharp look, and he closed his mouth.

My heart felt like it was in my throat as the guard led me down the red carpeted aisle in the center of the great chamber where the Patient Steward was hearing petitioners' pleas. I could see several people watching, and I knew they were wondering why this dirty group of travelers merited an armed escort.

But I didn't let that get me down. Instead, I met their eyes and smiled at them. Many of them smiled back.

When we reached the Patient Steward, I took a moment to study him. He had gray hair that was once black, and the wrinkles in his dark skin seemed to mark him as old, but there was a youthful glint in his eyes and an unfettered kindness in his smile that appeared to be ageless. It was as though the cruel ravages of time had left him unaffected—as if no sorrows had ever been able to dent his perception of the world. As I looked at him, I felt a pang of sorrow that I would be taking the reins of the kingdom away from this man who was so much more worthy than I to hold them.

"Well," he said kindly, "what have we got here? Travelers, unless I miss my guess."

The guard held out the sword he had taken from me. "This girl claims to have brought the Arm of Avalon, gentle Steward."

The Patient Steward's eyes widened. "Does she indeed?" He fumbled at his belt to remove the empty scabbard hanging there. "Well, give the blade to her, young man."

The guard hesitated. "Are you certain this sword is

the one, Steward?"

"If an old man's memory can be trusted, it *is* the one, but we'll soon find out, won't we? Now, hand this young lady her sword."

As the guard reluctantly—and with an obvious look of warning—handed the Arm of Avalon to me, the Patient Steward addressed the people congregated before him.

"Gentle citizens," he said, "we have here a claimant for the throne bearing what she says is the Arm of Avalon. If I can successfully unite her blade with its scabbard, then you shall be looking on your future queen!"

The crowd became utterly quiet, and the Peaceful Steward whispered to me: "What is your name, child?"

"Umm, Rapunzel Beauregard," I answered, flushing.

"Behold this swan before us, the young Rapunzel Beauregard," he said, flinging his arms out to the side, "and the friends who have assisted her in this difficult journey." Then he dropped the volume of his voice and smiled at me. "Now, gently slide the sword in its scabbard. You must forgive an old man's shaking hands—I'm excited, you see. I've been waiting for this moment for almost two decades"

Holding my breath and trying to ignore my pounding heart, I pointed the sword at its sheath. It slipped inside like butter.

The Patient Steward began smiling in earnest. "Behold your future queen!"

The people gathered before us began to cheer, and I could practically feel my ears turning pink. We had done it. Somehow, we had really done it.

CHAPTER 20:
SEEING RED

T o my surprise, the next few weeks were mostly a blur of activity. The Patient Steward—whose name, I learned, was Talon Redwing—really *was* as kind as he seemed. He was delighted at the prospect of planning my coronation ceremony and "infinitely glad" at the thought of relinquishing the throne once more.

A queen, I learned, had a surprisingly large number of needs. She needed attendants, she needed a large wardrobe, she needed to inform the kitchen of her culinary preferences, she needed to know the current state of court politics, she needed to know the name of this great figure and that one—and the list continued on, seemingly without end.

Talon was an immense help in cramming as much

of a royal Landdish education into my head as he could. He was more than happy to usher Poppy into her role as my attendant, and he even offered to find Thorny a spot as perhaps a guard or a knight-in-training. When I explained that Thorny was actually a prince and needed no such occupation, Talon began to fret over needing to prepare a banquet to welcome Thorny to the kingdom. However, I hastily assured him that such recognition wasn't what the prince wanted. Nice clothes and good chambers would be quite enough to satisfy him.

Unfortunately, the whirlwind of preparations and royal lessons meant I wasn't able to see Thorny very often. His mother also seemed to have disappeared again, but past experience told me she was probably somewhere nearby.

A few hours before the coronation ceremony, however, as Poppy was directing one of my other attendants on how to prepare my hair, it was announced that Thorny wished to speak with me.

When I heard his footsteps approach, I turned from the vanity to look at him. There was something solemn in his face, and I could tell he wanted to talk to me in private.

"Thorny," Poppy said warmly, stepping toward him and putting her hands on his chest. "I've been trying to find you," she said quietly. "I'd like to . . . speak with you."

The prince looked like he was going to be ill. "Poppy, st-stop touching me," he said, shoving her hands away. "If all the girls in the world but you fell victim to a plague, I—"

"Umm, Poppy," I said, interrupting Thorny before

he could say something he regretted, "I need to speak with Prince Thornwald alone. Perhaps you can talk to him another time. Can you and the others wait in the outer chamber while I speak with the prince alone?"

I could practically see the protests hovering at my attendants' lips—they needed to finish with their preparations, after all—and Poppy in particular looked disinclined to go, but my eldest attendant, Birdie, took charge: "All right, girls. Let's do as she asked. You know, I *was* wondering about the shoes we chose for tomorrow . . . ." And so she led them away, discussing the next day's wardrobe. Poppy gave one last calculating look at Thorny before she followed.

When the door shut behind them, I looked at the prince, who seemed to be avoiding my eyes. "How have you been?" I asked him. It felt almost like we had become strangers.

"Fine. I've been visiting Luna in the stables a lot. She's been missing you, you know."

I felt a pang of guilt. With everything that had been happening, I had forgotten about my beloved horse. What was happening to me? "Has she broken out of the stables or pastures yet?"

He managed half a smile. "A few times. I've left the city to visit Slate on occasion, too. He's fine as well, in case you wondered."

"That's great," I said, feeling guilty that I hadn't asked.

There were several seconds of silence that seemed to stretch into an eternity. Our breaths suddenly seemed loud, and I wondered if he could hear the thumping of my heartbeat. I felt certain I could have heard a mouse sneeze in that quiet.

Finally, I said, "Talon tells me that early tomorrow morning, we'll journey to the border, where I'm supposed to thrust the sword into the stone pedestal."

"Yeah," he said. "I did hear that."

"If you'll remember," I said slowly, "the man who removes the sword is to be my husband." It was ironic, really, that I had rejected Thorny when I could freely choose to marry a man. Now, however, I wouldn't have a choice at all.

He finally brought his eyes up to meet mine, and I was struck by the pain there. "Elle—"

"Miss Beauregard?" called one of my attendants timidly, peeking around the door that was now partially open. "Pardon me, but the Patient Steward needs to speak with you."

I looked at Thorny, torn and helpless, but he just waved a hand.

"I'll talk to you later," he said.

"All right," I said, watching him go.

Later, as I stood there, listening to Talon Redwing talk about coronation details while my attendants finished with my hair, I couldn't help but recall the stricken look that had been on the prince's face. What had he wanted to say?

The coronation ceremony began with a ball.

Per tradition, I stood up for the first dance with the Patient Steward. "Take it slow," he said, "for I *am* an old man—and I apologize ahead of time for stepping on your toes." But he was actually a very graceful dancer, and he ended up being one of my favorite partners.

After the dance with Talon, a man I believed had once been identified to me as a duke came up to us. He had brilliant red hair and a bright smile, but I found myself glancing at Thorny—who was skulking in the shadows—when the man approached. The Magnolian Crown Prince, I noticed, was glowering at the Landdish noble, though his mother was trying to speak to him. She had apparently decided to reappear for my coronation.

"May I have this dance?" asked the redheaded man with a bow.

I curtseyed and took his hand, smiling. "Of course."

After that, I danced with one noble after another. I kept expecting Thorny to step forward—was he a good dancer? I remembered how I had once said that the man I would end up loving would be someone who could dance with me—but he merely continued to glare at my partners.

When I was allowed a break from dancing, I tried to hurry toward him and his mother, but he stalked off before I got there. I frowned, looking after him. "What's wrong with your son?"

Queen Rose smiled. "Just a fit of jealousy. Don't worry about it." She took a moment to study me. "You look a little nervous."

"I am," I admitted. "But most of all, I'm famished. I don't know why the dinner has to be held so late. With everything that's been going on, I've barely been able to eat anything." And as the guest of honor, I couldn't sneak away to the refreshment table.

I saw Talon approaching, and I sighed. "I guess I have to go back to dancing. My feet will probably be aching tonight!" And then I was swept away once more.

Throughout the evening, I danced with many different types of men, but despite their attractions or kind words, all I could think about was Thorny.

The prince had been interested in me when I was a merchant's daughter, and he had still cared for me when I had been downgraded to a farmer's daughter. Perhaps everything had initially been rooted in my appearance, but I knew it had grown deeper. I *had* to speak with him. All he needed to do was pull the sword from the stone, and then we could have our happily ever after. Surely no one would deny me my first choice of who I wanted as a potential husband? I could make sure he was the first to try, couldn't I?

It was with these thoughts in mind that I danced and danced, and when the dancing was finally over, I wasn't allowed to rest, as it was time for the Reaping.

The Reaping was meant to be a happy time in which the Landdish people offered gifts to the queen in order of rank, with the nobles going first, then the wealthy landowners and merchants, and then the commoners. Usually, there were just a few representatives present from each village, not counting the nobles, and they gave gifts that were symbolic of an area or idea. Gifts might include crops or livestock from farming regions and clothes or jewelry from highly urban areas. The more expensive gifts tended to come from the nobility, of course, but I found myself appreciating the humbler presents more. Even then, however, the whole process made me uncomfortable.

What had I done to deserve this bounty besides request a sword from a mystical woman living in a lake?

When at last all the gifts were given, Talon Redwing began to initiate the next part of the ceremony. "Now that Rapunzel Beauregard has reaped the gifts of the Landdish people," he said, "she shall be crowned Queen of Airland." Someone moved forward with a beautiful silver crown on a pillow, and he took it and lifted it above my head. "I now pronounce you Queen Rap—"

"Wait!" a female voice cried out.

I looked up—heart pounding—and saw a black-cloaked figure being helped forward by a young woman holding a basket. As they approached, I realized the young woman was Nettle. But I wasn't sure who the old woman was.

When they climbed the steps and stood in front of me, I examined the stranger. Her face beneath the black hood was wrinkled and twisted, and I was struck suddenly by the impression that this woman had been through great sorrow. It wasn't until she lifted gnarled fingers and said, "Hand me that basket, Nettle," that I realized who she was.

As she grabbed the basket, she noted my look of surprise. "Didn't recognize your dear old stepmother, did you? All of my beauty is gone now. Of course, I suppose I don't need to tell you I regret my actions. But when I remembered you and your generous nature, I thought perhaps I could bring you a peace offering to make everything better." She lifted the basket, and I took it from her with shaking hands.

I scarcely knew what to say. Finally, I managed,

"I'm sorry for everything that has happened." I meant it, too. I looked down at the apples nestled in the basket, and my stomach growled. I was *so* hungry, and those apples looked *so* good.

"Come, child," said Iris. "You must be starving. Take a bite out of one of those apples. No one will mind, of course, if their beloved ruler sneaks a snack. Let this be the proof of our reconciliation."

I reached into the basket and lifted up an apple.

"Wait!" a voice said.

I raised my head and saw Thorny running up the stairs toward us. My guards moved to block him, but I told them: "It's all right. Let him through."

"Apples?" he said as he came to my side. "You can't trust anything given to you by this witch. I'll bet they're poisoned or have spikes in them or something."

While the majority of the people in the room couldn't hear Thorny, those near me could, and they began murmuring. My cheeks were warm with embarrassment. To insult a gift offered at the Reaping was considered highly offensive.

"Thorny, this is an important ceremony," I whispered fiercely. "You can't just barge into it."

"You know why she lost her beauty, Elle? It's because she cursed me out of my body! If she was willing to go to an extreme like that, do you really think she would try to make bygones be bygones by giving you a basket of *apples*?"

"Thorny—"

The prince snatched both apple and basket out of my hands. Apples flew out and began rolling all over the floor, and my guards grabbed Thorny.

"Wait!" I said before they could haul him away.

He looked at me in frustrated anger, and I asked him, "Can you prove it?"

I wasn't sure whether to believe him or not—was he just being paranoid?—but the best way for both of us to save face was for him to give evidence for his claims.

He wrenched his arms away from the two men holding him and growled, "I'm not some common criminal, so stop treating me like one!"

The guards backed off, hearing the animalistic quality of his voice, and he moved to pick up an apple. He handed it to one of the guards who had held him and said severely: "Cut into it."

As the guard did so, I noticed the expression on my stepmother's face become grim. Then I heard a gasp and turned to look at the apple. The inside was black.

A different guard put his fingers out to touch the fruit's toxic insides, only to draw his hand back with a hiss of pain.

"Cut open another," I said hoarsely.

While a guard reached for a different apple, Thorny pointed at Iris. "Guards, arrest her!"

Though most of the guards had their rifles in hand, they hesitated—the woman before them had been accused of being a *witch*, after all—and Thorny, impatient as ever, ripped one of their guns away and aimed it at my stepmother. "Arrest her!" he shouted, trying to fumble with the gun's safety.

Like the asp that strikes without warning, Iris drew a dagger. But unlike such a snake, Iris's target was not clear until it was too late to stop her. My guards moved to protect me, as did Thorny, but rather than contend with them, my stepmother twisted and drew her dagger across Nettle's throat.

Someone gasped—was that me?—and Nettle brought a hand up to cover the rapidly expanding red line on her neck. She gave her mother a look of pain and sorrow, and then she collapsed on the floor.

CHAPTER 21:
THE SERPENT

ears streamed down Iris's face as she crouched on the ground, holding Nettle in her arms. "I had hoped it would not come to this," she whispered. "But I have been left with no other choice." She kissed Nettle's forehead and then gently lowered her to the floor.

Rising, she said, "A curse! A curse on this would-be queen and her kingdom. I have now sacrificed that which was most dear to me—my beloved Nettle." She looked at Thorny with an expression full of malice. "You could've had this lovely flower, prince. She would have made the perfect queen. Instead, you must watch as the pathetic girl in front of you ruins this kingdom. My curse is this—one day, when Rapunzel is in the kingdom of Magnolia, she shall prick her finger on a thorn and die, and all of her kingdom shall perish with her. Just as the two of you ruined my life and family, so shall you do the same to each other. You can try to stay away from this girl, prince, but no matter what you do, my curse will still come to pass!"

With Iris's last statement, the curse must have hit me, as I suddenly collapsed on the ground, feeling as if some outside force had slammed into me.

"Arrest her," Thorny commanded my guards for the third time.

But then with a flash, Iris turned into a rat and began to run down the stairs and toward the exit.

"Catch that rat!" Thorny shouted, shooting his rifle only once and completely missing his target.

The great room was filled with screaming and recoiling. As if the rifle shot had not been bad enough to cause mass hysteria, no one wanted to be near a rat that was actually a witch. And so though Thorny initially attempted pursuit, it was in vain.

Growling under his breath, Thorny returned to my side and kneeled by me, holding my hand.

I stared up at him from the floor, my chest aching. I squeezed his fingers, and he tightened his grip on my hand.

"Rose!" he said loudly, calling for his mother. "Is there anything you can do?"

I hadn't realized Queen Rose was nearby, but I saw her suddenly appear overhead. She, too, got down beside me. "I can try," she said, "but we won't know for sure that it worked until the curse is enacted."

"But you can see the future!" he exclaimed.

"Yes, and there is more than one future to see," she

said impatiently. She began running her hands in the air over me and murmuring to herself.

I watched her, but my thoughts weren't easily focused. I felt shaken. I hadn't really wanted to believe that my stepmother was evil, but now it felt hard to deny. Or perhaps "evil" was the wrong word. After all, what mother would sacrifice her daughter for the sake of vengeance? That was more than just having a bad character; it indicated her mind was affected.

I tried to pull myself together and think of all the strains that had been put on Iris. My father valuing my beauty and my love above all, the loss of my family's wealth, the failure of Nettle to become queen, and the fact that I had caught a prince's eye . . . Nothing could justify murder, of course, but there had been a crazed look in her eyes that made me believe she had been pushed over the edge mentally.

"There," Queen Rose said. "I've done what I can."

Thorny assisted me in standing, and he gave me a worried look. "Do you need to go to your room?"

Talon Redwing, who appeared just as upset, said, "Yes, I can have someone—"

"No, no," I said. "Let's continue with the ceremony. People are frightened. We need to reassure them as best as we can."

Talon turned to look at the fearful faces—people had calmed down a little bit once Iris had left, but they were by no means serene—and sighed. "You're right. Let's continue. If we can."

In spite of the brave face I put on, I really was strongly affected by Iris's appearance, and when Talon placed the crown on my head, I could barely feel its weight. The crowd was unable to regain its pre-Iris energy, and it was all I could do to force myself to attend the lavish dinner Talon had orchestrated.

My appetite had ironically vanished, but I forced myself to eat anyway since I knew the next day would be a long one. Because it took several hours to ride from Starling to the border, we were getting up early in the morning. When we reached the pedestal, I was supposed to put the sword in the stone and then watch potential suitors try their hands at removing it. Afterward, we would camp there for the night. I didn't feel up for any of that, but I had to push on anyway.

I thought maybe I could find a way to talk to Thorny at the dinner, but he left early. Though I was surrounded by people, I felt alone when I saw him leave.

When I was finally able to go to my room after dinner, I was exhausted. Nonetheless, I sent one of my attendants to find Thorny. When she returned without him, I sighed and resolved to try to speak with him in the morning.

"I'm going to bed," I announced.

A chorus of "Yes, Your Majesty" answered me.

I nearly groaned. This being queen business really wasn't what I needed right now. Thorny was avoiding me, my stepmother had tried to kill me, and I was supposed to be ruling a country. What I wanted to do was cry.

Instead, I forced myself to think of my father's comforting voice as my attendants prepared me for bed. And then I slipped under my silk sheets and hoped for a dream about Thorny when I closed my eyes.

When I woke in the morning, I didn't remember a dream about Thorny. Instead, I felt exhausted . . . and my head hurt like it had been rammed by a dragon.

"Did you sleep well?" Poppy asked.

I started to respond and then froze. Poppy had been asleep when I had returned from the lengthy coronation ceremony, so I knew she hadn't seen what happened. I was glad she hadn't been there, but where *had* she been? Had the other attendants already caught her up on what had happened? Did she know her sister was dead and her mother a fugitive?

As I thought about Nettle, I couldn't summon tears, but I really was sorry about what had happened to her. She might not have ever been kind to me, but she *was* my stepsister.

"Birdie," I said, addressing my senior attendant, "would you take the other girls elsewhere to discuss what I am to wear for our ride? I want a moment alone with Poppy."

Laughing and talking eagerly among themselves, they left the room, though I saw a few of them give me curious looks as they went.

I had a long day before me, and the last thing I wanted was the conversation that was about to take place. But I had to tell my stepsister about what had happened. She *had* to find out from me instead of someone else.

"Poppy," I said, "where were you last night?"

She flushed bright red. "Umm . . . I was . . ." She sighed and bit her lip. "Look, I know you like the prince, but I like him, too, and I . . . well, I wanted to get him alone. So I skipped all the festivities and waited in his room for him."

I raised my eyebrows in surprise. "You . . . you what?"

"I waited in his room for him," she repeated, looking embarrassed. "I didn't get the reaction I'd hoped for, though. He pretty much threw me out immediately."

I looked away. Perhaps I should have felt a little irked, but with all that had happened, I couldn't. So I didn't push for more details. Instead, I asked her, "Has anyone told you about what happened last night?"

She shook her head. "The others seemed nervous about something, but they didn't want to talk about it."

It occurred to me then that I didn't have to tell her the full truth. She had to know her sister died, of course, but she didn't have to know it was at her mother's hand. If I forbade my attendants from discussing it and told Thorny and Queen Rose to keep quiet, then I could avoid imparting the most horrific part of the story.

But my heart knew that lying wasn't the right thing to do. Lying was a tangled web—what if someone eventually mentioned it to her? And what of all my musings on morality and being stained? A lie like this one would soil my hands for a long time—until Poppy's death or mine.

"Your mother and sister came to the coronation ceremony, Poppy," I said.

She gasped. "What? Where are they? Did Mother seem angry with me for becoming your attendant, or was she glad that I'm making something of myself?"

I felt like shedding tears for both Nettle and Poppy then. Life had of course been completely taken away from Nettle, but Poppy had been greatly affected, too. Threatening and cursing a would-be queen, drawing a dagger in front of her, and killing an innocent woman—all these things meant Iris would never be able to live a normal life. And Poppy might never see her again as a result.

"Your mother," I began, only to cut myself off. Then I tried again, "Poppy, your sister is dead."

"No," she whispered in disbelief. "That can't be. What . . . what happened?"

I turned away from her. My heart ached with empathy. "Your mother has always hated me. I know she has reason to, but I never imagined her hatred ran this deep. She wanted to curse me, and to curse someone, you have to sacrifice something important to you." I looked back at Poppy and saw the growing realization in her eyes.

"No," she said fiercely, "you're lying. My mother would *never* kill my sister."

I closed my eyes. "I wish I was lying. But you can ask anyone who was there. She pulled out a dagger, and—oh, Poppy, that's a horrible way to die." Opening my eyes, taking in the tears that were trickling down Poppy's cheeks, I started to reach for her, but she pulled away.

"Your mother is sick, Poppy," I told her gently,

225

thinking of all the signs that had been there. "Her desire for revenge has polluted her mind—"

"No!" shouted Poppy. "You're lying. My mother isn't a bad fairy. She's a good person. She wouldn't do that. You're just jealous because she never loved you! But she loves me and Nettle! She—" And then, tears streaming down her face like small bitter rivers, she fled the room.

I stared after her. Lies could bring bad things, but so could truth, couldn't it? Was there such a thing as a good lie? Should you stain your hands to prevent someone from feeling pain? Could it be selfish to give someone the painful truth so that you could feel that you remained unsoiled? Maybe morality wasn't as black and white as I wanted to believe.

The strain of the past few days made me want to break down and cry, but I didn't. Instead, I gathered my attendants, buried my emotions, and readied myself for a day of riding.

CHAPTER 22:
STONE HEART

n some ways, the ride to the pedestal at the border was worse than I had feared, and in some ways, it was better. Despite Talon's protests, I was allowed to ride Luna. But unlike the previous journeys in which I had been on her back, stops were discouraged, as each one meant that we had to find a suitable-sized area to rest the long trail of people and carts and horses behind me. We did make stops, of course, to eat and relieve ourselves, but the breaks were not as great in number as I would have liked, and we were all expected to maintain a brisk pace so that we could cover plenty of ground before night began to fall.

To further complicate matters, there were crowds waiting at different parts of our plotted path. The castle couldn't fit the whole kingdom at the coronation ceremony, of course, so some people waited outside in hopes of catching a glimpse of their new queen. I felt like a fish out of water, but I smiled and waved, and at one point, a red bird that I knew was Queen Rose landed on my shoulder to tell me I was doing a fine job.

All of my attendants were with me, except for Poppy, who was claiming an indisposition, so I didn't lack for company. Talon even frequently rode his horse beside Luna so he could tell me about this or that element of reigning over Airland. But the one person I really wanted to talk to—Thorny—was nowhere to be found.

Queen Rose told me that he was at the back of the procession, though I was unable to see him because of all the flags people were carrying. Furthermore, since I was expected to be near the front, I could not actually go to him. I thought of sending Birdie to fetch him, but I doubted he would come. For whatever reason, he was actively avoiding me. Queen or no, it was impossible to make Thorny do something he didn't want to.

Though my back was aching and my whole body felt exhausted, we at last reached the pedestal right before sunset. I dismounted amid trumpet calls with the help of Talon. My attendants had given me high-heeled shoes to wear which, while beautiful and made of pristine glass, were rather impractical for a day of riding.

It had begun sprinkling, to my dismay, but I attempted to look as dignified as possible while the Patient Steward led me up to the platform behind the pedestal. I noticed he seemed unaffected by the drizzle and wondered if that were a skill I would learn.

"Citizens of Airland," he called out, lifting his hands, "behold Her Beloved Majesty, the new mother of our people. She has proven she is fit to hold this throne, but she asks now for a man to prove himself worthy of standing at her side. We all know the strict requirements that a man must meet to slide the Arm of Avalon from the stone, so watch now as our queen places the sword in this pedestal, never to be removed unless by a worthy and selfless man."

At Talon's barely perceptible nod, I unsheathed my sword, which had been resting at my side on the whole journey to the border. I handed the sheath to Talon, who would keep it to test any sword that was claimed to be the Arm of Avalon, and then I lifted the blade into the air and brought it downward *hard*, hoping it wouldn't bounce off the stone and force me to tumble off the platform. But it slid into the pedestal with no trouble at all. In fact, it was all I could do not to fall forward when I didn't encounter the expected resistance. The crowd before me let out a cheer, and I took a shaky breath.

"People of Airland," I said loudly, hoping my voice carried into the crowd, "I have relinquished the Arm of Avalon, and whoever can take it out will receive my hand in marriage." I swallowed and said, "Men, I invite you to step forward and attempt to take the sword."

And step forward, they did, nobles and commoners alike. They formed into a line with a little jostling and laughing and probably even some boasting. Though the rain had picked up a little, it didn't seem to have affected the numbers of potential suitors that had turned out. I felt Talon put a hand on my shoulder, and I reached up and squeezed it, grateful for the gesture but unable to take any comfort from it.

Searching the crowd from the platform, I found Thorny and caught his eye, but then he turned away, and I knew with a deep ache in my heart that he would not try to remove the sword from its ornate holder that night.

Thunder rumbled in the distance, and I looked to the pedestal, where a man was sweating with the strain of trying to take the blade.

"Easy," said Talon kindly, "the Arm of Avalon will be instantly taken by the one meant to remove it."

The man gave a sheepish grin and shrugged before moving away to allow the next man to try his hand.

As every potential suitor approached the sword, I held my breath; and as every man failed, I released it. When at last we were hours into darkness, and I was soaked and so drained from this emotional event that it was all I could do not to collapse into a weeping heap, Talon said loudly: "If no other man wishes to try tonight, we shall conclude this ceremony and retire for the evening." There would be other men who would try, of course, but the ceremony requiring my presence would be completed.

When no one stepped forward, Talon gave a nod at me, and he began to escort me off the platform. Right before we went down the stairs, I paused and attempted to find Thorny in the darkness; when I could not, I continued onward with Talon. He took me to my large tent and kissed my cheek. "Do not worry, little bird," he told me fondly. Then, mistaking the cause of my anxiety, he said, "They will love you.

You shall see."

I smiled at him, trying to mask my emotions. "Thank you, Talon."

He gave a bow and then departed.

The servants had been busy during the ceremony, and everything was set up comfortably for me in my tent. My attendants wanted to take me out of my wet clothes and prepare me for bed, but I said, "No, not right now. Birdie, do you think you can find Prince Thornwald and . . . summon him to come to me? I need to speak with him."

Birdie hesitated. "Your Majesty—"

"I promise I will change clothes afterward. Please, go get him."

She curtseyed. "Yes, Your Majesty."

I watched her leave, and then, after dismissing my other attendants and telling them I would send for them eventually, I waited. I listened to the sound of the rain picking up and felt a pang of guilt that I had sent Birdie out in it. I wondered if she was angry at me or just considered it part of her duty. I was in such an awkward position. I knew what it was like to have servants, but after serving my stepmother and stepsisters, I felt much more sensitive to the feelings of servants—and much more reluctant to enlist their assistance. It didn't help that Birdie was old enough to be my mother.

I thought of the Magnolian tradition that required the heir to the throne to live among the people as one of them for three years—and the requirement that the heir be twenty-one to ascend the throne. The first served as a valuable lesson, and the second seemed only wise. I certainly didn't feel experienced enough with life to run a kingdom. How was I supposed to carry the weight of Airland on my shoulders?

At last, a drenched Birdie opened the flaps of the tent to come inside. Her wet hair was plastered to her head, and I felt another flash of guilt.

"I'm sorry, Your Majesty," she said. "His Highness, Prince Thornwald, is standing near the pedestal and refuses to leave, even though I told him you wanted to see him."

I took a moment to listen to the rain pelting the outside of the tent. I had been willing to brave the rain once for Thorny's sake; there was no reason not to do so again.

"Then I will go to him," I said, rising from my chair.

"Your Majesty—" Birdie protested.

"I must speak with him *alone*," I said. "Please go to sleep and tell no one about this."

"Your Majesty, I will wait to prepare you for bed," Birdie said stubbornly.

Some queens might have been annoyed at having their orders contradicted, but I smiled and shook my head. "Fine. But it would be smarter to get some rest." I opened the tent flap and stepped outside.

I had dried a little from the rain that had soaked my clothes earlier, but it had really started coming down hard since I first went into my tent, and I was drenched almost instantly. My four rain-soaked guards looked startled to see me, and I knew they intended to follow me, so I told them, "Stay here." At their uneasy expressions, I added with a smile, "What fool would be out in this rain?"

After taking a few steps forward, I nearly went back

to change shoes. The rain had turned the dirt to mud, and the heels of my slippers kept sinking down into it. But I doubted my attendants had packed anything more practical, so I continued on, trying not to wince as the mud oozed over the glass shoes and onto the tops of my feet.

I looked back at the tent briefly and saw that one of the guards was following me from a distance, though he was making a poor attempt to disguise his purpose. I shook my head and continued on, if a bit faster.

When I was fairly close to the pedestal, I could just barely make out Thorny, who was standing on the platform and staring at the sword. I moved closer and said his name, and he looked down at me.

"Are you going to pull the sword from the stone?" I shouted, trying to speak loudly so he could hear me over the noise of the rain. I walked up to stand beside him on the platform. "Why did you even come if you didn't intend to try?"

He said, "Elle," and then he fell silent.

"Or . . ." A thought suddenly occurred to me, and I looked at him, stricken. "Or did you try and fail?"

He shook his head, but he didn't look at me.

"Thorny, I've realized that what people think of me—whether I have power or the right amount of beauty—all that, well, it isn't important. What's important is happiness. And you make me happy, Thorny. My beauty doesn't mean anything to me. And this crown on my head? It . . . it puts us on an equal footing. But I've realized *that* doesn't matter anymore either. What matters . . . what matters is this."

I took in a deep breath. "I love you, Thorny. Will you take this sword and marry me?"

I waited for an answer, and it was like in that eternal moment all my senses were heightened. I could hear the low roll of thunder and smell the fresh scent of wet dirt. As I watched the rain roll down Thorny's face, I waited, wondering if he was going to refuse to answer, wondering if a bolt of lightning was going to suddenly come down and strike us both dead.

And then he said, slowly, his lips bunching up together and his tongue lightly releasing the word with deliberate finality: "No."

"What?" was all I could manage. I felt like I had been frozen in place, both my body and mind refusing to do everything they had been doing for years like a trustworthy horse that unexpectedly balks at the reins. That word—*no*—resonated in my head, bouncing around inside my skull as if suddenly my whole world had been simplified to include that word and that word alone.

"I don't love you," he said, each word ground out like bullet shells to fill the emotional gun he was pointing at me. "Your beauty has always been your most important feature to me, and if you lose it by marrying me, you'll be nothing to me. If you're foolish enough to think I've cared for you, you're wrong. You're just a stupid girl with a pretty face. I don't know why I ever tried pursuing you. All I've ever wanted since I first saw you was your body. It's only now that I have been able to realize that you aren't worth all the trouble I've gone to." He gazed at me blankly, as though he had suddenly become only a shade of the man he used to be. And then he said, "Leave me, fairy."

I turned without a word and started to run. I barely

made it a few steps before one of my shoes sunk into the mud and my foot slipped out. But rather than pause to pick it up and put it on, I left the shoe there and fled with one foot bare.

The rain that fell from the sky mingled with the tears running down my face, washing them away and hiding them, perhaps, but doing nothing to clear away the pain I felt.

I rushed past the guard that had followed me, and he exclaimed, "Your Majesty!"

But I didn't speak—I just kept running. When I reached the tent, I paused briefly, panting, and then went past the three uneasy guards with only a trembling nod.

Birdie and my other attendants, who had rejoined her, all flocked around me, toweling me off and helping me change into dry clothes. One of them commented on my missing shoe, but I was too busy trying to hold back tears to speak.

When at last they helped me into bed—what a pathetic figure I must have made then, needing help with something so trivial!—I sent them away from my tent, telling them I would have a guard come get them when I needed them in the morning.

Birdie ushered the other girls away like a mother hen, and then I was alone. Or so it appeared.

As I wept into my hands, I heard a gentle voice say, "Rapunzel."

I looked up and saw Queen Rose standing there. "R-Rose," was all I could say, and she moved forward to kneel beside me and pull me into an embrace.

I cried in her arms. I don't know how long. But it was almost like having a mother again, and though my whole world felt as if it had shattered, at least I had that small amount of comfort.

When at last I was composed enough to speak—if not unbrokenly—I pulled away a little and asked, "Why does it . . . hurt s-so much?"

She looked down at me with a sad smile and said, "Because he wanted it to. But you mustn't believe him. He simply lacks faith in himself. Loving my son can't always be easy, but it's worth it. Hold on to your love."

I took in a ragged breath. "You—you really can see the future?"

"Yes," she said, giving me another hug. "I really can."

EPILOGUE

I did as Thorny's mother advised me. I locked my love for him away in my heart. I still ached inside, but I had been given a kernel of hope.

There was certainly enough to keep me busy. Talon continued to advise me, and Poppy pushed past her grief enough to return as one of my attendants.

But it was hard learning to be a queen of a foreign kingdom without having had any formal training, even with Talon's help. I had forgotten how tiring the drama of duchesses and earls could be. It was especially difficult to grit your teeth and give lavish gifts to some of the last people you believed deserved them. But despite all the kingdom's liberal leanings—such as having a woman as the primary holder of power and expecting any man who married her to take her last name—a queen was expected to keep her court content, lest the nobility decide it was in their best interests to revolt.

Talon compared the nobility to fine china—you were expected to polish it and fawn over it and treat it gently, but really all you wanted to do was put it away and eat off your everyday dinnerware.

To compound my problems, no one had any success in locating my stepmother in Airland, and I suspected she had escaped to Magnolia, where I had no jurisdiction. She likely intended to simply wait for her curse to take hold, but a part of me still worried that she would reappear in my court with another batch of poisoned fruit.

Having a gaggle of attendants was nice since I never lacked pleasant company, yet Talon warned me not to become too familiar with them, as they could not be wholly trusted not to accidentally spill their queen's secrets. I thought that was a rather cynical thought, but I took his recommended approach to heart, though it meant I often felt alone, even when in company.

A few months passed by, and I listened eagerly to any scrap of news on Thorny. Much of what I heard managed to feed that kernel of hope even as it made me despair. And then one day, I was trying to help solve a dispute over rights to a stream when a man entered the throne room. I recognized him instantly as one of my information-gatherers. In his hands was a bloodied scrap of clothing.

"Your Majesty," he said as he rushed up the stairs to stand before me, "I have just spoken with some of your soldiers. They say the King of Magnolia and his son were attacked by a vicious beast while hunting along the border. And I . . . I have some terrible news."

My hands gripped the armrests of my throne so tightly they turned white.

END BOOK TWO

THE SMOTHERED ROSE TRILOGY
CONTINUES ...

BOOK 1: THORNY

In this retelling of "Beauty and the Beast," a spoiled boy who is forced to watch over a flock of sheep finds himself more interested in catching the eye of a girl with lovely ground-trailing tresses than he is in protecting his charges. But when he cries "wolf" twice, a determined fairy decides to teach him a lesson once and for all.

BOOK 3: ROSEBLOOD

Both Elle and Thorny are unhappy with the way their lives are going, and the revelations they have had about each other have only served to drive them apart. What is a mother to do? Reunite them, of course. Unfortunately, things are not quite so simple when a magical lettuce called "rapunzel" is involved.

ALSO BY ONE GOOD SONNET PUBLISHING

ACTING ON FAITH Though Mr. Darcy has no assurances of Elizabeth Bennet's regard after she rejects his proposal, he moves forward in his quest to secure her hand. Unfortunately, neither Caroline Bingley nor Elizabeth's childhood friend Samuel Lucas will make it easy for him.

OPEN YOUR EYES Elizabeth Bennet is forced to reevaluate her opinion of Mr. Darcy when Mr. Wickham contradicts his own words. In the course of her dealings with the two men, she realizes that first impressions can sometimes be deceiving.

WAITING FOR AN ECHO, VOLUME I, WORDS IN THE DARKNESS When Mr. Darcy comes to Hertfordshire to decide between two prospective brides, he has no idea that his eye will be caught by someone so much lower in consequence than him as Elizabeth Bennet.

WAITING FOR AN ECHO, VOLUME II, ECHOES AT DAWN When Elizabeth travels to Kent, she meets Mr. Darcy's prospective brides and faces the consequences of two tragic events. Can her feelings for Mr. Darcy conquer the machinations of a former love interest?

For more details, visit
http://rowlandandeye.com/

ABOUT THE AUTHOR

Lelia Eye was born in Harrison, Arkansas. She loves reading and misses the days when she was able to be a part of the community theater group in Harrison.

Lelia has enjoyed writing since she won a short story contest in the sixth grade.

She now lives in Conway, Arkansas, with an adorable toddler, her husband, three dogs, and two cats.

To see the blog she shares with Jann Rowland,
please visit:

http://www.rowlandandeye.com/

CPSIA information can be obtained at www.ICGtesting.com
Printed in the USA
LVOW08s0821170215

427234LV00018B/595/P